The Bra shifter rules

Always put your mate before yourself.

Respect another shifters' mate.

Do nothing to expose the existence of shifters.

Do no unnecessary harm to shifters or humans.

Respect all nonhumans.

She looked at him over her shoulder. His blue eyes seared her with heat. The intensity of his stare made her shiver. Lifting one hand, he laid his fingers against the blush of her cheek. Then he wrapped his arms around her from behind. He buried his nose in her hair and let his wolf rumble in satisfaction. "I'm ready to show you off at Julia's whenever you are."

"Let me check my face and hair. It'll only take a minute." She returned a few minutes later looking amazing.

Her hair was pulled back in a fashionable messy bun. A single strand was left loose to fall down the side of her face to the tip of her breast. He longed to follow that strand to its destination, scrape his teeth against her nipple and inhale her precious scent.

She was without a doubt the most beautiful creature he'd ever seen in his life. Rose placed her arms around his neck, and he relished how her warmth seeped into his body.

"I may have to change my mind, you look too good, and I'll be forced to kill some idiot who tries to dance with you."

She rolled her eyes at him and grabbed her purse. "Come on, Romeo, I'm ready for a boat ride and a turn around the dance floor."

Simon held her hand as she got into the boat then jumped in and revved the motor. "I'll go slow so I don't mess up your gorgeous hair." He winked.

She blew him a kiss and fluffed her hair dramatically.

Even going slow it only took twenty minutes to reach the pier serving the bar. He already heard the music and boisterous patrons. He cut the motor and helped her exit safely; boats weren't designed for high heels.

Rose looked up and down the line of boat slips and shoreline. "Where's her sign?"

"She doesn't have one. We'd rather random humans didn't wonder in. Mates are more than welcome, but the occasional human to happen upon the bar isn't very well received."

He led her to an open table. "I'll get us drinks, would you like wine or a whiskey Coke?"

"A whiskey Coke sounds great." Her eyes were bright with excitement as she checked out the crowd.

He squeezed into an open spot at the bar and waved over his cousin. "Julia! How are you, cher?"

"Oh, mon dieu! Simon, it's so good to see you. I heard you found your mate."

"I did." He gestured to their table. "Rose is seated right there, stop over if you get a break."

"Oh, elle est de toute beauté. You're a lucky man, cuz."

"Don't I know it." He grinned. "Can I get a Whiskey Coke and a beer?"

"Oui."

He turned his back to the bar to check on Rose. Simon's breath caught as she unconsciously moistened her lip with the tip of her pink tongue. That mouth was made for sin, with its plush lower lip. He imagined her mouth doing wicked things to a certain part of his anatomy. Blood thrummed in his veins. Simon turned to inconspicuously adjust himself, his faded jeans were suddenly way too tight. Her intoxicating scent of coffee and cinnamon rolls licked at his groin even from across the room. He wanted to rub himself all over her, saturating her with his scent whenever they were in public. His wolf wouldn't be satisfied until they were mated.

Gazing at her across the room his blood surged, he imagined her naked on his bed, her thighs parted in invitation. He lowered his head and tasted her passion. Loving her long into the night, her excited cries entwining with his hoarse groans as they made the bed shudder and shake. He shook his head. He really needed to get control of his randy thoughts. This was date night and he would show her a good time away from his bed for once. *Down boy,* he snarled at his wolf. When he glanced at her again she was snickering and shaking her head at him. He must be imagining loudly.

"Here you go, no charge, and congratulations, Simon." Julia rapped her knuckles on the bar top before she turned her attention to making another customer's drink. She was very busy, so he left her to it. He'd barely taken his seat when the band took the stage for another set. He stood and held his hand out to Rose. "May I have this dance?"

"Why, yes, you may," she said playing along.

Simon held her close enough to see the sparkles in her blue eyes. He loved the way her gaze lit up when she was happy. But his wolf itched to see her eyes dazed with passion as he made love to her, and then sated and sleepy afterwards. For now holding her on the dance floor would do. Rose's intoxicating fragrance surrounded him, teasing his senses. He was in heaven.

He cupped her cheek with a large, warm palm. "I'm so happy you moved into our house, Rose. Having you in my arms makes me the luckiest man in the world." The moment she agreed to move to his house he'd called it *their* home. His glowing blue eyes regarded her with a tenderness that made her breath hitch.

She tightened her arms around his neck, urging his face closer to hers. "I didn't want to go back to Anna's, to an empty bed anymore," she told him. "If you really plan to have me as your mate, it only made sense."

"Just say the word and I'm yours completely. Forever." He smiled, then dipped his head, kissed her deeply and nuzzled her.

OUTSTANDING PRAISE FOR V.A. DOLD AND HER NOVELS

Simon's story takes us back to the bayou and the hot brothers looking for their mates. Simon however is a special case. He has some issues. Issues that stream from not having that personal connection when serving our country proud!!!!! Then of course there's an underlining issue......someone doesn't want him to mate?!?!

Simon is strong and HOT as all get out of hell, he is just broken. Broken beyond anything his family or friends can fix. He knows he needs help and he feels that there's hope when his sister in-law simply touches him. Still that's just NOT enough...not until she touches him....not until.....Rose.

Rose...a beauty, in Simon's eyes. Not your average skinny size heroine. No way...this gal has got you're curves and lack of self-confidence that goes with it. A foster child since a baby, the only real family is the one that she claims her own. That would include Cade's mate Anna, her boys and her two foster brothers. However, like everyone else...she has a past. One that she's not even fully aware of yet (it's amazing what brothers will do for their sister). I'm personally on the border with Rose for a long while through this story. I toss back and forth even if she's worthy of Simon. Thankfully, I'm no Goddess...right...LOL

As their feelings progress, outside a ploy is being sought to prevent them from becoming a mated couple...I know ...WTF!!!!

It's totally freaking CRAZY!!! Awesome fight scenes though...I totally LOVE Simon's reaction when he hears about the first attack...Priceless...LMAO!!!

The Final fight scene...OMG...now that one...it was one that was totally a read twice and absorb!!!! Maybe read again!!! OMG!!!!

Rock Him!!! Rock Him!!!

Wholly Boogers!!! I just realized I didn't say one word about the love scenes between Simon and Rose...What was I thinking....they were H-O-T!!!! Notice I put the word *love* and not *sex* because between them that's the only way to describe it...just fyi.

I totally love what Simon and Rose plan to do for the future...that's AWESOME!!!!

This story really takes you for one heck of a ride...your intrigued...upset...curious…sad...over joyed...then you're like ...OK...WHO THE HELL really wants the throne!!!

BJ Gaskill   5 stars

Normally I don't do reviews, but the book was so good that I had to do it. Since I read my first Rubenesque story, I haven't gone back. I search for bbw books all over the net, buying and reading them like candy. Love my heroines with real attitude, real appetite like me, and if is a shifter story that's better! Very enjoyable story that I know I'll read again and again in the future. This is an ongoing series being 6 additional brothers, friends of Cade (vampires and other shifters) and 2 of the Heroine's sons. I so can't wait to read Simon's story (emotionally wounded ex-marine and Cade's brother) and Etienne (Cade's friend - Vampire Lord). First book I read from this author and definitely will not be the last.

Zamanta De Jesus   5 stars

Billionaires, romance, and shifters oh my! I loved this book. This is the first book I have read from V A Dold and I must say it was excellent! I couldn't put it down! And I can't wait to read more.

melanie a ramey   5 stars

The woman is REAL - plus sized – fluffy

PicardsMom350 5 stars

This book kept my interest from beginning to end. It was a love story with Family and just the right amount of humor and love with some suspense thrown in. I would recommend this book to my friends and family. I can't wait for the next book from this author about the Le Beau Brothers.

Audrey Carpenter 5 star

When the others come out I will buy them! I love the idea that the woman regresses to about age 25 and the body returns to that age also. Interesting idea.

Donna Turner 5 stars

Amazed me how their love grew stronger with each breath I took. When they finally found each other my eyes filled with tears and my heart filled with the desire to know that kind of love from my mate, the man of my dreams.

I haven't read a book about shifters in quite a number of years and now I can't remember why! V.A. Dold has rekindled a deep love from my past with her dynamic writing in Cade. Her words wove their way through my mind and my veins and I became part of the story instead of just a reader.

Patricia, Room With Books 5 stars

Holy mother of OMG! As most know, I don't read shifter books. Yes, I know that I'm one of the few so when I come across one that I never wanted to end, I will shout it from the rooftops.

Brian's Mom 5 stars

ISBN-13: 978- 978-0-990523512
ISBN-10: 0990523519

Print edition June 2014

Dedication

Thank you to all my readers and fans of the Le Beau Series. I appreciate you more than I can say.

Thank you to my friends and family who cheered me on and believed in me even more than I believed in myself.

And thank you, Tina, the best editor a girl could ask for.

...You helped make this all possible.

Simon

Le Beau Brothers

By

V.A. Dold

Prologue- The Plan

Emma Le Beau knelt in front of her altar as she prepared to take her daily meditation time and speak with the spirits when the Goddess came to her. "Simon has suffered much, more than any of my children should ever endure. His mate is Rose, a friend to Anna. She will be here at the plantation for Thanksgiving. Her love and connection to Simon will be the final thing he will need to return fully to his human form. I've set events in motion to guarantee Simon's mate will come. Take care, my daughter, blessed be."

Bursting with excitement, Emma ran to Isaac. "I've been given another mate's identity. This woman is meant for Simon."

Isaac's brows furrowed. "Why Simon and not one of the older boys?"

Taking Isaac's hand Emma quietly said, "Fate doesn't work in chronological order. There's nothing type 'A' about fate. Fate does what it wants, when it wants, where it wants, and to whomever it wants. You can't control or dictate fate, it just is.

"The Goddess said our sons would receive their mates at the proper time and then she would disclose to us who that mate was and where she would be found. She never said our sons would receive their mates in order by age from oldest to youngest. We should simply accept the gift she has given and not question her." Emma kissed him, so thankful for her own mate.

"I can see the reasoning behind Simon receiving

1

his mate before Stefan, he's still so withdrawn from his experience. I'm thankful the Goddess wants to ease his suffering by bringing him his destined mate. Especially if she is the answer to complete his healing. It's killing me to see him suffer and not able to help him." Isaac drew Emma in as close as he could get her.

Nibbling on her fingernail, "We need to come up with a plan to get Rose here," Emma said almost as if speaking to herself. "The barbecue is tomorrow and Anna will be here. I'll bring up her friends and family from Denver. If I can get her to mention Rose, I'll point out that Cade's house is very large and has plenty of room for visitors."

"So, plant the seed and let it grow?" Isaac searched her face. "Do you think that will be enough?"

"The Goddess said she would come. I'll simply give her the idea for the invitation." Emma's smile was blinding.

Rubbing his hands together, "This is happening so much faster than I ever dreamed possible. We came up with the idea only a few weeks ago," Isaac said. "When we first planned to help all seven boys find their mates I was sure it would take years. Our Goddess is moving this along nicely. Once Simon sees Rose and experiences the draw of one mate to another, the unique scent one has for the other, nature will take its course."

Isaac let out a loud belly laugh. "I guess I don't have to worry about the boys going through their long lives without experiencing the incredible love that is enjoyed between mates. Now if we could only get some grandchildren."

Emma sighed wistfully. "I saved many of our

baby things from when the boys were born. I would love to hand them down to my grandchildren."

"You can be very devious, my love." Isaac nodded in approval. "Okay, it's decided. I will leave the laying of bread crumbs to you." He nibbled on her neck and all thoughts of plans flew out the window.

The first mate disclosed had been Anna, Cade's beautiful mate. Isaac and Emma were thrilled with the results of helping Cade meet his mate. All they had to do was arrange for Cade to meet Isaac for lunch at the Crescent City Brewhouse and then cancel at the last minute. That left Cade free to have a long leisurely lunch with Anna. The love affair and happy ending took off from there. Sure there was a bump or two in the road but what great love hasn't had them. Harassing ex-husbands, dangerous crime bosses, and suspicious adult children have nothing on a Le Beau.

Chapter 1

AT WAR

Four years earlier

Simon Le Beau squinted at the never-ending dunes, another mirage shivered in the distance as his transport crested a ridge. His squad was returning to base after a tour of recon. Just driving to and from the base, they had to be careful to stay in the tire tracks packing the sand. Following what had proven to be a safe passage in a world full of IEDs and ambush parties. *Home sweet home,* he thought as he looked at the base, which was really just row after row of desert-tan tents. In a moment of madness, he wanted to splash paint onto everything to break up the monotony. *When the recruiter gave me his rah rah speech he should have told me I'd be eating, sleeping, and breathing sand.*

Within minutes the guys had poured from the transports and scattered across the base. Habit had him in his tent removing his gear, he wiped his weapons clean and buffed his boots. It was a constant battle against the layer of grit that tried to encase everything. Extending his arms over his head, he stretched unused muscles and flexed stiff joints. Riding in a vehicle that lacked any form of shock absorbers for hours was cruel and unusual treatment. Finished cleaning, he relaxed on his bunk and read a magazine.

Simon: Le Beau Brothers

His attention was focused on what he was reading, when a shiver ran up his neck. Tremors of unease came from the direction of the village a few miles to the north. This was the first time he'd felt anything other than alertness or boredom since he had arrived two months ago. His friend Peter was part of a team ordered to drive through that seething town to collect a VIP coming in for a high profile inspection of the base. Based on the emotions emanating from the soldiers of the team, they were becoming lax in their diligence. It'd been months since shots had been fired and the lack of aggression was affecting the soldiers and creating a false sense of security.

He sat up, dropped his magazine to the mattress and scratched his fingers through his military cut. Limited options presented themselves. *Ah hell, I thought I could get through this without telling anyone.* There was no way to explain the situation, without disclosing his gift. He wasn't sure how his squad leader, Mark Anderson, was going to react to him saying he could sense people's emotions and dispositions.

An hour later Mark sat forward and leaned his elbows on the table. "Are you a nut? One of those crazy new agers?" Scratching his chin, it was clear Mark wouldn't take him seriously without proof. Calming his mind, Simon opened himself to sense the room. A soldier in the far corner was on the verge of some kind of violence. A group of four marines were hassling the man as they often do. Some saw it as a rite of passage while others saw it as bullying.

Simon touched Mark's arm to get his attention. "Do you see that soldier by himself in the corner?" He tipped his head that direction.

Mark looked at the corner Simon had nodded toward. Without speaking, he quirked an eyebrow at Simon.

"He's going to lash out at that group about five feet to his left. I estimate in about thirty seconds." Simon said in a bored tone of voice. He was making a point and meant for it to make an impression. For additional effect, he counted down as he felt the man's aggression rising. "Ten, nine, eight…" When he got to one, the soldier launched himself at the group tormenting him.

Mark's expression took on a whole new level of interest in what Simon had to say. He listened to the situation as Simon laid it out. Without a word he clapped Simon on the back then left to meet with his superiors.

Swallowing hard on a dry, sandpaper like throat, Simon wondering what this meant for him now that he'd put himself out there, swinging in the wind.

The sun caused him to squint and shield his eyes as he returned to his bunk not sure what else to do. He had just opened his magazine to finish the article on tuna fishing when a Private summoned him to Major Patterson's headquarters at the center of the base. Not more than twenty minutes after he had spoken with Mark. *Well, this is it, either they believed me or they are sending me for psych evaluation.*

Simon entered a plush office by desert standards.

His boots sounded loud against the flooring. He glanced at the oak bookshelves stocked with a variety of bestsellers. *I'd love to borrow a few of those*, he thought wistfully. Major Patterson waited, tapping his fingers on a massive oak desk. *Give him a crown and he would look like a king in that leather chair,* which looked very suspiciously like a throne. He steepled his fingers as Simon approached and eyed him like a bug in a jar.

"Private, I'm told you have some kind of sixth sense radar for trouble," Major Patterson said without preamble.

"Sir, I guess you could call it that. All I know is I can feel people's emotions and sense the temperature, so to speak, of a situation."

"So, you are saying you can 'feel' something's going on in the town that we are unaware of?"

"Yes, Sir."

"You also 'feel' the relaxed nature of the team that will be driving through said town, and are of the opinion there's to be an ambush of some sort."

"Yes, Sir."

"I'm supposed to hand down orders based on your 'feelings,' is that right?" Major Patterson used air quotes and sneered as he said *feelings*, like it was a dirty word.

"No, Sir, you need to do what you feel is right. I felt compelled to cover my fellow marines as best I could. In this situation, that included informing my superior of the level of aggression I sensed in the situation. What is done with that information is up to people with a pay grade higher than my own, Sir."

"You're dismissed, Private." Major Patterson waved his hand toward the door as if he were shooing a fly.

Simon saluted the Major, ignoring his wolf's snarl, and went back to his bunk, utterly defeated. Just for one moment, he'd hoped to make his superiors understand and listen. But he'd put himself on the line for no reason and his friends were still in grave danger. He'd reached a new low and was in desperate need of some form of skin-to-skin contact to calm himself and his wolf.

He wasn't used to being in situations where he had such complete lack of control. Snarling and raging, his wolf wanted to take matters into its own paws. Flopping on his bunk, he rubbed his temples to relieve a headache that was building. *The next four years of service are going to be a living hell and my only objective is to survive and come out in one piece, mentally and physically.*

The next morning, Simon vaulted upright in his sheet tossed bed. The sound of revving engines woke him with a start. He rolled from his bunk to squint at the staging area through still sleepy eyes. The most heavily armed vehicles on the base were preparing to move out.

He stretched his sleepy muscles and yawned. *What's happening that I haven't heard about?* It was hard to keep a secret from a man with superhuman wolf hearing. As he made the military corners on his bunk's bedding, everyone in the barracks began preparing for the day.

Checking his uniform for military perfection, he adjusted his collar. Satisfied with his appearance, he was ready to face the day. Today he had practice at the shooting range. The newly assigned marines would be there for hours. Experience taught him to eat a solid breakfast and hydrate well before joining the soldiers to begin shooting. *First stop, the canteen.*

Last thing he wanted was to qualify as a sharp shooter. Shooting a man unarmed and unaware was not his style. His empathy would destroy him if he did that to another living being. A fully aware and threatening opponent was a completely different story. Aiming carefully, he made off center shots to guarantee he would remain in his position within his unit. Not making changes was just fine with him.

A complete lack of concentration aided him in achieving less than stellar accuracy. The squad leader looked at his used target and shook his head. "Private Le Beau, I don't see sniper status in your near future."

"I can accept that if you can," Simon said as he grinned at his friend.

They both laughed as they trudged back to the barracks for cool showers and fresh uniforms.

Relaxing in his tent, Simon heard the VIP convoy as they returned. The squad had been expected two hours ago. It was late and the last rays of sunlight were waning. He rushed to check on his friends, the stress of worrying all day had been excruciating. "Sir, how'd it go?" he asked as he skidded to a stop next to the lead truck.

"You were right, Le Beau, There was a band of insurgents entrenched in town. Without the warning, we would have been blindsided. The injuries and loses could have been staggering."

"Were there any injuries, Sir?" He took visual inventory of his friends as he waited for an answer.

"Yes, but only minor, we made it through without anyone sustaining major injury of any kind. We have you to thank." He clapped Simon on the shoulder and headed to Major Patterson's tent for debriefing.

He breathed a heavy sigh of relief, the team and VIP were all alive. He assumed someone in the chain of command had heeded his warning. Mark could not have commandeered the heavy transport without their command. Thankfully there were no casualties. He'd at least kept his friends safe. He stood with hands on his hips watching the team drive to the back of the base. *I'll accept that as a win,* he thought as he raised his eyes to the sky in silent thanks.

Simon scrubbed his boots, giving them a good spit shine. His squad was relaxing around him in the barracks. Lights out was in ten minutes so everyone was winding down. The sight of Squad Leader Anderson as he came through the door had everyone scrambling to attention. Simon stood rigid at the end of his bunk with the rest of the privates.

Mark stopped in front of him, surprising not only him, but also everyone in the squad. Simon had a reputation of keeping his head down and avoiding trouble. But no one ever made the mistake of thinking he couldn't handle himself in a fight. The opposite was the case, they respected his fighting abilities and also his desire to avoid confrontation.

"Private Le Beau, I have transfer orders for you."

At first Simon looked at him a bit dumbfounded. *What's going on? Are they dishonorably discharging me? This is the payback I get for putting myself out there?* "Sir, where am I being transferred too?"

"You'll be a part of a special unit that consults the base on a variety of matters. You're being transferred from the team, not from the base. Major Patterson wants to speak with you tonight and then you will be assigned a desk starting tomorrow," Mark told him as they approached the Major's office door.

The short walk from his tent to the Major's office felt like miles. He didn't want to be separated from his unit. His entire body broke out in a sheen of sweat and his pulse raced. *This must have been what walking to the gallows felt like.*

Entering, they both stood at attention and saluted.

"At ease, men. Private Le Beau, is the example of today's success something I can expect from you in the future?"

"Sir, I can't guarantee success. But I can give you and the men the advantage of preparedness. I can tell you what I sense from an area, but I won't be able to give you specifics such as exact number of insurgents. Although, I can tell if it is a large or small number of people but nothing exacting, like a body count."

"That's more than we've had before. Come to my office at ten hundred and bring coffee. We will discuss how best to use the benefit of your 'gift' then." He ran his fingers across his baldhead. "This is all new ground for me, don't make me look like a fool, Private."

"I will do my best, Sir."

"Dismissed." He saluted Simon and Mark then they turned to go.

Early on, the upper directive recognized the value and advantage Simon offered with his gift. He could evaluate the level of a squad's readiness and the threat level of any area. He was used like a Geiger counter. When the leaders needed intel on an area regarding troop placement, Simon was sent in under heavy guard to sense the situation and evaluate the threat level.

Not long after he was transferred to the special *Consultant's Squad*, a squad of one, Major Patterson summoned him again.

"Le Beau, I am promoting you to Special Adviser. You will be my personal tactician, reporting only to me," the major announced.

From that day forward, Simon was protected more heavily than any VIP visitor. Major Patterson didn't want his goose that laid golden eggs in harm's way.

Chapter 2

Skin Contact

Drumming his fingers on his desk, Simon couldn't shake the anxious feelings plaguing him. He was three weeks short of his first year anniversary in the service and his symptoms began to alarm him. He'd known for some time that he was reacting to the lack of touch and skin contact. In a world filled with marines and little else, he had limited ways to satisfy this particular shifter need.

Rubbing his hand up and down his thigh, he tried to still the sporadic twitch that had begun two days prior. It started as a small quiver, so slight, it was easily hidden. Now it was much too noticeable. If he didn't find a creative way to fulfill his shifter needs for touch and physical contact, he was going to be in serious trouble. A Marine doesn't get touchy feely with his fellow men.

He looked up as he heard the office door open. A new Marine he hadn't met smiled and handed him a flier. A huge smile broke across his face as he read the announcement, he was in luck, a serviceman's appreciation dance was being held Saturday night in the rec hall. Perfect, this was exactly what he needed. The rec hall was nothing fancy but it was functional. It was really just an extra large tent with a solid floor. As he read on, he honed in on the bottom line. The women from the base as well as nurses from the military hospital would be there. He had every intention of dancing with all of them if he had any say in the matter.

Simon was going to dance and enjoy himself for the first time in almost a year. The women for the most part were attractive both inside and out. Problem was, dating within the ranks on his base was discouraged. He was denied his one possible easy option for contact, up until now anyway. He'd watched the women closely, getting a quick sniff whenever possible. A wolf never knows where or when his mate will appear. So far, no luck in the love department. But through his observations, once they shed the drab military colors and severe hair requirements, they became quite fetching.

Glancing at his watch, it was time to head to the rec hall. The dance was scheduled to begin at nineteen hundred hours. He wanted to be at the door as they opened, there wasn't a minute to lose. Whispers could be heard as he passed small groups of women, the ladies were naturally drawn to Simon's literal animal magnetism. He hadn't even selected a table for himself when the first nurse approached him for a dance. Back home in Louisiana he'd made it a point to not take advantage of the young ladies who would flock to him, as they did to all his brothers. Using that kind of control over an unsuspecting human female was just wrong as far as he was concerned.

He was walking his fourth dance partner back to the table when he sensed the disgruntled emotions coming off his friends. They mistakenly perceived Simon dancing with every woman as hogging all the available attention. That wasn't what he had in mind at all. To smooth their ruffled feathers, Simon steered a small group of lovelies to his friends sitting at a table in the corner. "Gentlemen, I would like you to meet a few of the ladies here tonight." He introduced each, one by one. "Ladies, please join us, I'm sure these gentlemen would love to ask you to dance as well." On his suggestion, the level of discord lowered dramatically.

As the DJ began the next song, Simon stood and offered his hand to the lady sitting nearest him. He was on the dance floor relishing the contact of a woman in his arms. At every opportunity he ran his hands up her arms. Slid his palms along her exposed skin. It was like a feast for his wolf's soul. As he walked to and from the dance floor, changing out dance partners, he made it a point to hold their hand. If he sat a song out, he had a lady perched on his lap. He was soaking up the contact, storing it away like a camel stored water.

The DJ finished the final song, signaling the end of his night. Simon felt great. It was a total recharge to his wolf's soul. He may have found a solution to his problem and he just might make it through his remaining three years without too much discomfort. He prayed there would be dances on a regular basis.

Over the next six months, things went well. He had just filled his first cup of coffee from the pot in his office when the anxiety returned. He'd kept it under control, no twitching or spasms for almost a month. His hopes to hold out until another social were dashed. Before he'd had the opportunity to recharge with a dance or social, the twitch returned more severely than before. Frantically Simon shoved reports off of his desk calendar. There had to be something he could attend.

Dismay flooded him, the next dance wasn't for another four weeks. Rubbing his jaw with his palm, he searched for a solution. He couldn't chance waiting that long. Luckily, he was on rotation for a weekend pass that coming weekend and between now and then he would think of a way to make it work to his advantage.

He stared at the clock, willing it to read sixteen hundred. It was finally Friday and he had a forty-eight hour pass burning a hole in his pocket. The spasms had gotten so bad his right knee bounced like a nervous teenager at his first prom. 'Click,' the hour hand struck four p.m.

Simon shot out of his chair and almost ran for the door. He'd researched the town for options. There was a massage parlor in the American section and that would be just the thing the doctor ordered. It only took thirty excruciating minutes to get to town and locate the parlor. He jumped from the Humvee. "I'll meet up with you fellas in a few hours at the bar."

"See you in a few," they hollered as they roared away.

A tiny bell tinkled as he opened the door. *Wow, they actually post their services on the wall like a fast food joint.* Surprisingly, unlike the United States, here you could buy that *happy ending* right out in the open.

Up there. On the price menu. In black and white. He was reading the offered services and prices when an elderly woman came from the back room. Thankfully, she wore a nametag, Naba. Simon wasn't here for sexual favors, he needed a set of hands on him for as long as he could get them. According to the list of options, massages were available by the half hour or hour. He glanced away from the wall to who he assumed was the manager. "Naba, how many hours of massage can I get immediately?"

She stared at him wide eyed for a moment. *Aw, hell, I scared her.* He quickly opened his wallet to show he had money. Held it towards her as a sign of good faith. The sight of his bulging wallet had her pulling her hand from the security alarm. *Whew, that was close.*

In broken English she said, "Three hours all I have today."

Simon grabbed the edge of the counter as his legs went weak. The thought of three solid hours of hand to skin contact had him trembling.

Naba yelled to the back room curtain. Within seconds, three frightened young women emerged. Speaking their language, she must have explained what he wanted. Their expressions turned to warm smiles and the closest took his arm.

He passed through the curtain to an inviting back room. Automatically he scanned the space for danger. Not a threat to be found. The soft candlelight and incense soothed his wolf almost as much as the hand on his arm.

Each of the lovely women gave him a one-hour massage. The oils used felt amazing on his skin. As he was leaving, Naba allowed him to purchase a small bottle of the oil, some candles and incense. He would find a way to use them and stay within his marine regulations.

Head held high, he heard the little bell tinkle again

in farewell. The past three hours had been one long continuous massage. Simon was now the parlor's number one customer.

The next morning as soon as breakfast was over Simon excused himself and returned to the parlor for another long massage.

The ladies loved him. All he wanted from them was a good old-fashioned massage with no extras required. He was tucking his shirt in, as he emerged from behind the curtain. Every woman lined the reception area. The tallest woman, Mysha, approached him. "Mister Simon, please come back. We want to massage you everyday."

"I would love to come here everyday, sadly I cannot. I can only promise to return as soon as I have another weekend pass." With a warm smile, he touched each woman's arm as he walked to the door.

Reluctantly he tossed his knapsack into the back of the Humvee before he joined the squad returning to base. It was back to the grind for all of them.

Settled into his desk, he breathed in the aroma of his fresh cup of coffee. He hadn't even gotten his first sip when Major Patterson called him to his office.

"Le Beau, do you have a distance limitation on your human radar?"

"Yes, Sir. I have experienced that ten miles is the maximum distance I can sense."

"I need an area twenty miles east evaluated." He

rubbed his baldhead absentmindedly. As if mumbling to himself, "I need to make sure you're out of harm's way." His scalp was turning red from the scrubbing he was giving it. "Can you sense through metal?" He eyed Simon like a bug again.

Simon cupped his chin and rubbed his fingers across his lips to hide the fact he was trying not to smile. "I can sense through anything, distance is my only limit."

"You will stay inside a tank for maximum coverage. That, or God forbid you might be hit. A squad I can replace, you I can't. Your squad will move out at twenty hundred hours. I want stealth, you will only go twelve mile east and sense the situation from a distance."

Oh man! I tried to protect my squad and I've put them in even more danger. They are going to be on the frontline every time I'm sent out.

"Be at the staging area at nineteen thirty. I will brief your squad leader. I expect to debrief you the moment you return from the operation."

Simon found it a bit embarrassing that he was required to ride inside a tank, but his Major wouldn't take the chance that he'd meet a bullet up close and personal. Inside the armored tank it was almost impossible for him to incur an injury.

He sighed as he walked with the squad to load up. His friends didn't understand why he was relegated to the inside of a tank and ribbed him incessantly.

"Hey, Le Beau, do you need help getting into your booster seat?" one of them jabbed.

"Sure, I could use a diaper change too," he shot

back. If you can't beat them, join them. He hoped the ribbing would end quickly.

An hour later Simon joined Mark in Major Patterson's office. "Sir, there is a small band of fighters eighteen miles east. The aggression level is medium to low. I would guess they are forced enlisted who are trying to avoid combat."

The Major was silent as he processed the intel. "Good work, Le Beau. The squad will be off duty tomorrow. Anderson, I want you here at ten hundred. Dismissed."

The squad fell into a routine, night excursions to gather intel followed by a duty free day. Within a week the ribbing about his tank rides ended. They appreciated the intel he provided. The men knew many of them would have been injured or dead without Simon's unique ability.

A month later

Simon and his team were on a recon mission to an area twenty miles west of base. "Halt!" he yelled over the roar of the engine. Everyone stood silent, awaiting orders. Simon may not be the squad leader but he ran the show when they were on a mission.

Something is very off in this area, he couldn't quite place what it was but it was not friendly. The men were on high alert. Utilizing hand signals he sent scouts out under the cover of darkness.

The enemy was hunkered down in a pile of rocks west of their string of vehicles. Simon studied the situation thoroughly to verify the aggression level. If he ordered a sloppy hit on civilians, his gift of empathy would make him suffer horribly. Satisfied, he guided his men in. On his signal the small hive of fighters were hit with mortars. Once the debris cleared, Simon took a minute to scan the area.

Exhaling a breath he didn't realize he had been holding, he called all clear. He gave a silent prayer of thanks to the Goddess. Another mission completed without injury or casualty to his men. It was a heavy burden to bear for one man, but he felt he had to do what he could to keep his friends safe. He never considered the cost he was paying with his control and his wolf.

Simon tapped his pencil on the desk, *I need skin contact, as quickly as possible.* The spasms and anxiety were coming more often. After several months of ops, he noticed the more missions he went on, the more insurgents he was responsible for killing, the further he slipped into himself. As his need to seek out human contact became more and more often, the effects became obvious. Fighting his wolf for control had become more difficult. And the massages weren't sustaining him as long as they used too.

He worried he was going to turn wolf in the middle of the base. He shuddered like a junkie in withdrawal as he lay in his bunk that night. He dreamt of a lovely dove gray and white wolf with cute little tan trimmed ears. She had the most stunning eyes, the kind that look right into a man's soul. She captivated his wolf.

Night after night, the female wolf quietly trotted into his dream and lay next to his wolf. They never romped or played. They just lay as close as they could, touched each other as much as possible. The nightly specter calmed his wolf in ways Simon had never been able to. Without her visits, he would have never survived his last year in the service.

He lovingly drew a life like color image of his wolf angel. On his next weekend pass, he went to the only tattoo artist available. He prayed the man had some talent as he showed him his rendering. One of his massage friends agreed to be his interpreter. "Can he do it?" Simon asked.

She spoke with the man for a minute then answered, "He can do it but it will take several extensive visits to draw the wolf and add all the layers of color. He has a book of past artwork he can show you if you want to judge his work."

That was perfect as far as Simon was concerned. He could memorialize his savior wolf on his back and get extensive skin-to-skin contact at the same time. Win-win in his book.

He was riding with his squad for their weekend in town. He had used every pass he received over the past few months to complete the tattoo. The art was impressive and covered the majority of his back. Some of his friends thought it was rad, others thought he'd gone a little loco. But Simon knew the truth of it and that was all that mattered. The wolf and the time required getting the tattoo saved his life.

Simon sat on the edge of his bunk. He was hiding

in the barracks. He had only days until his final discharge after four long years. The Major had tried every trick in the book to get him to reenlist. He didn't have a clue there was no way that would ever be possible. He breathed heavily with his eyes closed. It took every ounce of effort and deep concentration to fight the shift his wolf was trying to force. He kept his hands hidden in the folds of the blanket he sat on so the other soldiers couldn't see his hands shift from human to wolf and back again. Finally Simon wrestled his wolf under control.

Simon and his unit were assigned to scout an unfamiliar sector. He stretched his senses as far as they would go. Something had his radar on high alert but he couldn't pin point the problem. It was like a strobe flashing but in the guise of emotional energy. One second it felt aggressive then BAM! It was joyful. He halted his unit and signaled Mark over.

"Sir, I sense something but it's extremely erratic. I can't pin point if it is a threat or not. I've never felt anything like it."

"We'll have to investigate the old fashioned way then." Mark signaled the unit into recon formation and put them through the drill they knew so well.

Moment's later gunfire erupted and chaos reigned.

An enemy cell high on the local street drug, wildly fired upon the unit. Most of the men were able to find cover, Mark wasn't so lucky.

The battle ended as abruptly as it began and Simon sensed the enemy moving away. A medic field dressed Mark's leg as they swiftly prepared to move out. They needed to get him to the hospital ASAP.

Simon blamed himself for his best friend's injury. He should have known the threat was there. *Why didn't my gift work this one last time?* Try as he might, the answers didn't come.

He visited Mark to check on his progress. It didn't matter how many times Mark told him it wasn't his fault, that he'd given the order so he was to blame, Simon didn't hear it.

The struggle with his wolf worsened with each passing minute until Simon didn't know if he could hold him back any longer. He had twenty-four hours to maintain human form and then he would be in the clear. It proved to be the longest, roughest, twenty-four hours of his existence.

He gritted his teeth in concentration. *I can do this, just a few more steps.* Slowly he exited the transport plane to the tarmac. He shook with the effort. He held his human form, but barely, until he was safely in the back seat of his parents' car. Headed home to the plantation, he lay silently in wolf form.

Emma Le Beau took her mate's hand as tears slowly tracked down her face. Her baby was suffering, and she couldn't help him. At least not until she understood it. If anyone could help Simon it would be her. She needed to speak with the spirits and devise a plan to make him whole. She wanted her Simon back, no one said no to Emma when she was determined.

Chapter 3

Simon's Recovery

Simon emerged from the forest as his wolf. Closing his eyes, he raised his head to the warm sun and cooling breeze. It didn't help, the ache in his chest remained. Opening his eyes, his gaze zeroed in on his personal home. If he concentrated really hard, he could imagine his mate walking along the porch, waiting for him to return. A familiar yearning filled him, the desire for his one true mate. When would he find her? Was she living close by or in another country? He'd found a modicum of peace in shifting and going for long runs. But it didn't fill his need.

He was restless; the feeling had hounded him for a while. There was no understanding it; it just was. Shifting to human, he walked across the expanse of lawn nodding to himself. He was going to do it, he would enlist for a four-year stint today. Perhaps the physical aspects of Marine life and the travel would bring him some peace. If the Goddess was in an especially good mood, he might even meet his mate. He sure wouldn't find her sitting at home.

Isaac shook the wolf sleeping on the sofa. "Come on, Simon, you really need to try to be human more. You are shedding like a husky in the summertime." Isaac sounded exhausted.

With a start, Simon woke from the dream or should he call it a nightmare? That fateful decision led to his present condition: every time he attempted to shift to human, it felt like being a hundred feet below the surface of the ocean, he could see a sliver of light but not reach it.

Someone stroked his fur in slow rhythmic glides. It felt like heaven and helped slightly but wasn't enough. At this rate, it would take two years before he could shift back.

As they say, hindsight is twenty-twenty. If he'd known joining the Marines would be tantamount to a jail cell for a shifter, he would have never enlisted.

I now understand why we don't have jails as a system to reform shifters. You can't lock a shifter away from others and expect a positive outcome. Put a shifter into a cell and he'll waste away and become lost in his wolf form. Shifter law had two solutions for crimes depending on their severity. For breaking a lesser law: always put your mate before yourself, respect another shifters' mate, and respect all nonhumans, there was the sentence of blood rights. A brutal and barbaric ritual where the criminal was tied to a stake and the offended party beat him to within an inch of his life.

For the unforgiveable crimes of exposing shifters to the world or harming another shifter for any reason other than self-defense, the sentence was death.

The only exception to this simplistic system applied to the royal family, a crime against the royals was death, period.

After an hour of attempting to shift, he harrumphed in disappointment. A few weeks had passed and he'd hoped there would be more improvement. He desperately wanted to meet Cade's mate at the barbeque today, but he couldn't make it to the surface. His repeated attempts left him exhausted and he now lay on the couch napping.

Drifting in and out of dreams, he jolted awake as pain, like an icepick in his temple, shot through his skull. His moans of agony came out as whines and whimpers.

In addition to being stuck in wolf form he had almost no control over his empathy. If he had hands he would be cradling his head. This was bad! There were too many people here for the barbeque and he was in emotion overload. No longer able to block or filter emotions as they struck him, he was battered unmercifully, and damn it was painful. He could handle a few people at a time but this exceeded his limits. This was a migraine times a thousand.

Was that a female's voice coming from the kitchen? he wondered through his haze of torment. Pressing his eyes shut tightly, he heard soft footfalls cross the room and smelled the sweet scent of woman.

"Hello, Simon, I'm Anna James, Cade's mate. May I touch you?"

He couldn't speak in this form even if his head wasn't cleaved in half. Instead, he made a small harrumph sound and opened his eyes. It took a second to focus, she had squatted next to the couch about ten inches from his face and waited for his permission. With only paws available, he couldn't shake her hand. Doing the next best thing, he reached forward, stretched his neck toward her, and licked her cheek. His wolfy hello made her giggle. He loved the sound of a woman's laughter. She tentatively began to pet him, and scooted a little closer.

Simon rumbled, this woman's caress brought a sense of peace and health he'd never experienced in all his one hundred and seventy years. It felt like his energy level had been jump-started. The surge had his human half rising closer to the surface. It was as if his human soul was stretching and reaching toward her touch.

She stroked him and scratched behind his ears. *Oh my God, that is amazing!* Her hands felt so good. His wolf continued the soft rumble of satisfaction in his chest. As close to a purr as a wolf could get. He adjusted his position on the couch, he needed her to touch every inch of him. *Please, Anna, don't stop what you're doing.*

He heard his father calling for everyone to be seated and she whispered, "I'll come back after dinner if you would like." With one last scratch her fingers were gone.

His human half shot to the surface like a bullet from a gun, her touch was nothing short of a miracle. Clutching the doorframe for support, he rounded the corner into the dining room. A hush fell over the family as all heads turned toward him. Anna had her back to him and slowly turned to look him in the eye for the first time. The short few steps from the doorframe to her chair were like struggling through quick sand.

He extended his trembling hand to her, after so many days unable to speak, "Welcome, Anna," was all he could croak out. His throat felt dry and raw from disuse. She gave him her hand and remained very still as he raised it to gently brush his lips across her knuckles. He turned to Cade as he released her hand. "You have a lovely mate, brother. She's a treasure." Already, the exhaustion was returning. He gritted his teeth, determined to remain human until he reached the couch. His backside hadn't even warmed the cushions before he lost control to his wolf again.

Twenty-five minutes later, he heard her soft footfalls and scented her as she returned. She lowered herself to sit cross-legged on the floor next to him. He sniffed for Cade's scent, concerned that his brother would resent this interaction with his new mate. He didn't smell or sense anxiety or jealousy from his brother, rather the fresh scent of pride.

Her healing magic was profound, even his wolf sat silently watching in awe as this human woman achieved what no one else had. Somehow, just her caress was healing him. He didn't understand it and he sure as hell wasn't going to question it. If her touch helped him rejoin the human world, he would accept every stroke with relish and find a way to thank her later.

It felt so good to lay with his eyes closed and absorb whatever she was doing. He felt her instinctively reposition her hands strategically on his head and chest. From her shaky, hesitant fingers, he would bet money she was unaware of the way she intuitively reached for the perfect position. A shifter's wolf resided mainly in his thoughts and heart, a virtual second soul in the body. She had unerringly located his wolf within without realizing it.

He started his low contented rumble again and relaxed under her hands. Wherever she touched, he felt a mild heat, it seemed to radiate from her palms. The sensation was warm but not overly hot. It felt REALLY good. She remained still for such a long time he started to doze off.

Like a heating pad that had shut off, slowly the warmth stopped radiating from her hands and the areas she touched cooled. He waited for her to pull her hands away before he rolled off the couch and lowered himself to the floor next to her. Expressing his gratitude, he laid his head in her lap for a moment, gave her hand a little lick, then rose and padded down the hall and out of sight. His body and soul urged him to sleep and absorb the healing it had taken in. He could almost feel it soaking into every cell and molecule.

He woke the next morning still in wolf form but feeling amazing. His human soul was closer to the surface, that sliver of light was a little larger and brighter. If he could skip as a wolf, he would, maybe do a cartwheel too. *I sure hope she comes back today. Damn, shifters really need opposable thumbs in wolf form.* He cocked his head, studying the doorknob. With no other choice, he waited and prayed for her return. This of course left him time to review what had happened the night before. He gasped when he realized that once she stroked him, the pain in his head disappeared. He hadn't noticed the spike being removed from his brain. He'd been too busy enjoying her touch.

Two hours passed, he was losing patience and preparing to shoot through the door the next time it opened so he could track her down. That's when he heard them approaching the patio door.

"You can do this, cher, just follow your instincts like you did last night."

"I'm afraid I might hurt him. What if this energy shooting out of my hands is harmful if I zap him too much? I have no idea what I'm doing or how to do it."

"My mother said you're a natural healer. Do what feels right and it will be fine. She said technically you don't need training. You instinctively do what is needed for the injured person. So training will be a bonus but isn't essential."

"Learning from a real gypsy who is also a voodoo priestess is going to be so cool!"

Cade laughed as he held the door open for his mate. They both stopped just inside the door as they came face to face with a very excited Simon. He rushed forward and rubbed himself across her legs. If Cade hadn't steadied her, Simon would have pushed her over in his exuberance.

"Hey, calm down, you've got her covered in hair," Cade groused jokingly.

Anna was laughing so hard she slipped and landed on her rump in the kitchen. Before Cade could help her stand, Simon had her straddled and was licking her face happily.

"All right, all right, that's enough, remove your wolf tongue from my mate or lose it."

Simon jumped back and crouched playfully, tail wagging wildly.

"Do you want me to try to heal you more, or would you rather take a run with Cade?"

He sat so fast he almost bent his tail. That would have hurt, a lot. Panting, he waited for her to tell him what to do.

"Okay then, healing it is. Do you want to use the couch or the floor? I might be able to reach around you more easily on the floor."

Simon chuffed happily and led them to the center of the living room. He unceremoniously laid himself out in the middle of the room and waited, tail thumping against the wood flooring.

He watched as Cade shook his head and took a seat in the corner chair. Anna was a little tentative as she figured out where best to sit and place her hands. The moment she settled on a position, he felt the energy flow from her hands to his body. He let out a huge sigh of relief and began to rumble. She gradually moved her hands around his body until her arms were wrapped around him, holding him in a gentle hug.

God, it felt so good to be held when he felt like a pile of miss matched parts and pieces instead of a complete wolf or man. He had always been in control, strong. The person everyone depended on. But that man had slowly faded week by week, minute by minute. Until it was an effort to just remember to breathe.

Shifters thrive on touch. Craved skin-to-skin contact. A need so common and easy to fulfill that you take it for granted. If you sat back and watched a room full of people carefully, you could pick out the shifters quite easily. They are the ones touching this person's arm and then that person's shoulder. Running their palm down a friend's hair.

It had never occurred to him when he enlisted in the marines that a simple thing like touch and contact would be as scarce as water in the desert. When a soldier was stationed in the U.S., it was fairly easy to find human or shifter contact but put that soldier male or female into boot camp, on a ship, or overseas for deployment and something so freely given was a rare commodity.

A human can handle the lack of contact fairly well and learns to adapt. A shifter suffers horribly with no way to get relief or feed the need. He gets by in the beginning with a feeling of mild annoyance like when you think you have forgotten something but can't remember what. Then it grows into a mild hunger that no amount of food will assuage. Gradually it develops into a gnawing that slowly drives the shifter into severe depression.

Simon had been discharged from the Marines in a state of deep depression. When he first returned home he'd slept all day waking only to eat. Through almost constant touch, stroking, cuddling and contact with family and shifter friends he was now able to function fairly well. He was still very quiet and withdrawn but he improved every day. It was rare to see him without someone touching him in some manner.

His whole sense of self had faded until his wolf was the only thing that held him together. So he had turned inside in order to survive. Through the love and staunch determination of his family combined with the encouragement from his wolf to rejoin the world, he was becoming the man he once was. Now, he had Anna too.

She spoke softly as they sat together on the floor for over an hour. She told him about herself, her sons, anything that came to mind.

Repeating the night before, her hands cooled, signaling she was finished for the day. As amazing as the energy felt it also wore him out. He gave her his wolfy thank you of a lick to the cheek and wondered to his bed for a nap.

The three of them fell into an easy routine. Every day he moved a little closer to the surface. Four weeks later he was able to shift and hold his human form for a short time. From that day forward he was able to hold his human form a little longer with each session. As Anna studied with Emma she learned to use the tools of a natural healer. Every few days she added a new aspect to her process, not only did she use energy, but she now incorporated herbs, crystals, and essential oils.

He could now shift for ten or fifteen minutes several times a day. He waited for Anna to remove her hands before he shifted. "I know I've said it before, little sister, but thank you."

She smiled warmly at him. "I love helping you, although I sometimes think I get more out of it than you do."

He cocked his head. "How so?"

"When the energy moves to you it isn't coming from me, it is flowing through me. The best way I can describe it is, I'm a conduit or tube, funneling the energy to you from a very powerful source. But just as you get the perfect amount of energy, I also receive what I need to be the best healer I can be."

"Really? I didn't realize that, I thought it came from you." He frowned and looked to Cade for confirmation.

He shrugged. "Mom says the same thing, it comes from somewhere else."

"Huh. Well, wherever it's coming from, I'll take it. I'm going to take my nap. You guys want to go for a run later?"

Cade took one look at Anna's excited expression and said, "We look forward to it." He grinned and led his mate to the door.

Chapter 4

Thanksgiving

The sound of tires on asphalt and car doors closing heralded the arrival of Rose. Cade gently touched Simon's shoulder. "Simon, I'm sorry, but could you please shift to human? Anna's friend is about to walk through the door."

Stupidly, he had exhausted himself trying to be human before Anna's friend arrived. He put everything he had into shifting before she came through the door, which left nothing for interacting. He would just have to rest and use what little energy he had to not suddenly pop into wolf form and freak out the human.

Everyone turned as the front door opened. Isaac, Emma, and Rose walked in loaded with suitcases. Hearing the commotion, Anna hustled out of the kitchen, wiping her hands. She couldn't believe what she was seeing! Both women squealed, grabbed each other and started a hugging dance combination.

Reluctantly Anna let Rose go from the tight hug she had her in, wrapped her arm around her friend's shoulder, and they both turned to face the room full of handsome men and her mother-in-law. "Rose, you know John and Thomas, and you've already met Isaac and Emma. This extremely handsome piece of male specimen is my husband, Cade."

He stepped forward, taking Rose's hand in both of his. Clasping it gently, he said, "Rose, it's a sincere pleasure to meet you. I'm so glad you're able to spend extended time with us."

"I'm glad I was able to come. I hated to miss the wedding. I'm sure the service was beautiful."

Simon's body jerked as if trying to rise and go to that beautiful, musical voice. He was concentrating so hard on maintaining his form he hadn't really heard her voice with his ears but his soul had reacted. Strange.

"I wish you could've been here as well, but we can make up for it now." She gave her friend another squeeze. "This scoundrel is the second oldest of the family, Stefan. Stefan, this is Rose. The one with impeccable manners is Marcus. Marcus, please meet Rose."

Each of them stepped forward and gallantly kissed the back of Rose's hand as they strangely leaned in, and she swore they sniffed her.

Anna gestured to Simon lying with his eyes closed on the couch. "You remember I told you about Simon. He's not feeling well, but wanted to join us today. He'll come to the table for dinner if he's feeling up to it, otherwise I'll set a plate aside for him for later."

Rose O'Leary's gaze was transfixed on Simon. Without thinking, she walked to the couch where he lay. *God, I want to run my fingers through that head of hair... What the heck is wrong with me!?*

Try as she might, she couldn't shake the intense desire to pet this stranger. Like a ravenous stray dog that hadn't eaten in a week, she raked her gaze down his delicious body. The way Anna had described him, she had imagined a big, bulky, stern military man. Like the incredible hulk, without the green. Instead, he was a feast for her voracious eyes, blond thick hair, a bit shaggy as it grew out. He had delectable wide shoulders and lean hips.

Even though she pressed her nails into her palms to suppress the urge, she found herself reaching out and gently touching his shoulder with her fingertips. The caress was really barely a touch at all still the electricity zinging between them was palpable.

Stunned by the sensation and her own actions, she surreptitiously drew her hand away. She was mortified and wanted to run for cover, but touching him had somehow cemented her feet to the floor. It had felt like coming home as her fingers had stroked the few silken strands. At least that is what she imagined the feeling of coming home would be like when she read her novels and watched movies like "You got Mail." A fierce surge of protectiveness rushed through her. *MINE!....*
Where the heck did that thought come from? The shock of her intense reaction almost made her stumble backwards.

She kept her face down and eyes glued to the floor as she returned to Anna. Chewing her lower lip, she examined what had just happened. It was surreal, as if she were watching another woman take charge of her thoughts and actions. A new, confident, self-assured Rose, had invaded her mind, body, and soul the instant she laid eyes on the silent man across the room. It scared the living crap out of her.

Simon: Le Beau Brothers

***

Anna Le Beau watched in shock as her friend acted completely out of character. Rose was normally very shy and introverted, always flying under the radar. But *this* Rose, was completely different, she had touched a strange man in front of a room full of people she had just met. Rose NEVER touched men and certainly did not act confident unless she was wearing a power suit and running an extravagant event. Her two personalities were a mind-blowing dichotomy. Breathing deeply, Anna smelled confusion and fear rolling off her friend. As Rose had drawn close to the couch, Anna saw Simon's head raise slightly and turn toward her. His nose seemed to twitch but as Rose retreated he'd returned to his original position.

Now, isn't that interesting...Cade, did you just see that?

I did, do you think....?

Maybe...

Leaning toward Rose she whispered, "Are you all right?"

Rose took her hand and encouraged her toward the privacy of the kitchen. "I don't know. You know me, I don't just walk up to strangers and touch them like that. Why did I do that?" she asked.

"Don't worry about it, hun. Let's enjoy the meal and we can talk tonight after everyone goes home. I don't think anyone was watching anyway," she said to comfort her. She knew darn well everyone had seen Rose's reaction to Simon but she wasn't going to tell her friend that.

Pulling the pies from the oven, Anna wiped her hands on her apron. "Okay, everything is set. I'm going to change for dinner, why don't you sit with Thomas and John in the great room."

A few minutes later Anna appeared back with the others. "If everyone will move to the dining room, dinner is ready. Emma and Rose, would you please help me bring the food to the table?"

As everyone settled into his or her seat, Anna held the carving knife out to Isaac. "Would you like to honor us by carving the turkey?"

With a happy little grin Isaac inclined his head and accepted the honor.

Once the platters were loaded with sliced turkey, the feast began as steaming bowls and platters were passed around the table. Everything was perfect. The turkey was juicy and succulent, the mashed potatoes were rich and creamy, and Anna's family recipe for hamburger dressing was the absolute hit of the meal.

Rose watched her friends and the Le Beau family, quietly taking it all in. She was thrilled to see Anna so in love, and her new family was genuinely inviting and had accepted her as if she had always belonged.

Seated across from Stefan, she smiled as he eyed the mashed potatoes fiercely.

"Do I have to share these?" he asked Anna.

Anna laughed. "Take as much as you want, there's more in the kitchen."

Rose recalled the last time she had been part of a family dinner such as this one. It had been over a year ago when Anna had asked her to join the family for Christmas. She had still lived in Denver and was waiting for her final divorce decree. That celebration had been just the four of them, Anna, Thomas, John, and her. Being a part of this celebration struck home exactly how much she missed out on as an orphan. Wistfully she mused, *what would it have been like to grow up in a family like this? At least I was lucky enough to have Jack and Michael as foster brothers. I should call them later and see how their Thanksgivings went.* She could tell already she was really going to like these people.

She was drawn from her thoughts when the room filled with moans of delight as the men finished eating.

She chuckled to herself as Stefan scooped a third helping of potatoes and gravy onto his plate. He didn't seem to care that dessert was being served.

Anna announced, "I made my family's favorites, pumpkin and strawberry rhubarb. I hope you like them," as she returned from the kitchen carrying pies.

Thomas and John both said together, "Oh, yeah, Mom's strawberry rhubarb pie is the absolute best."

With the pies relegated to the pages of history, everyone sat back in their chairs, and there were quite a few waistbands being loosened.

"We'd like everyone's attention for a minute." Everyone quieted and waited to hear what Anna had to say. "Why don't you tell them, babe?"

"Mom, Dad, in about six months you'll be grandparents," Cade announced.

The cheering was deafening with everyone congratulating them.

Thomas and John high fived. "Is it a little brother or little sister, Mom?" John asked.

"We don't know yet, hun, I'm not sure if we want to find out ahead of time."

"Rose, do you think you'll be able to stay long enough to see my baby into the world?" Anna asked.

"You couldn't keep me away."

Isaac smiled with heavy lidded eyes half closed with satisfaction. He stole a glance in Rose's direction and gave Emma's hand a gentle squeeze under the table.

Rose smiled, thrilled for Anna and watched the family talk excitedly about the new baby. She harbored a few concerns about her friend having a baby at her age, she could discuss that privately with Anna later.

Dinner was cleared away and the party relocated to the great room. The area filled with activity: loud, boisterous men doing what men do when you get a group of them together.

During dinner her heart felt achy, empty, and she had wondered what the heck was wrong with her. Absently, she had rubbed at her chest to ease the strange sensation. As she trailed behind the family to the great room the sensation eased. That strange yet familiar draw that had ensnared her earlier, tugged at her again. As if a thread were tied around her heart and soul and someone were drawing it in.

Taking a much closer look at the man across the room, she wondered what it was about him that seemed so familiar. She felt as if she recognized him in an almost elemental way. The sudden feeling of somehow knowing this complete stranger was both exciting and confusing. There was no possible way she could know this man and yet it felt like she had known him her entire life. *What the heck? This is just plain freaky.*

Tucking her long blond hair behind her ear, she tried to put her finger on it. The intense lure felt so familiar and yet she couldn't pinpoint where she had experienced it before. She felt like she was grasping at smoke. It was like a dream she couldn't quite remember mere moments after waking.

Deep in thought she hadn't seen Stefan walk toward her. She gasped in surprise. *Holy cow, he's quiet, he about gave me a heart attack.* He wriggled his way between her and Anna, before he wrapped one arm around her. He winked at her and Anna, which had Anna shaking her head and rolling her eyes.

The almost inaudible gasp from Rose ricocheted through Simon Le Beau like a fire alarm in the middle of the night. He went from what everyone thought was a catatonic state to full alert as he shot to a sitting position. His nose rose to sniff the air, twitching from the tingle of an amazing scent. Tendrils of shock and surprise rolled at him in waves from the beauty Stefan had his arm around. HIS beauty. HIS MATE.

His glare held a violence his family had never seen him exhibit. Death lived in that icy stare. He kept his hands low, hidden from Rose's view, as they shifted into the deadly claws of his wolf. He struggled to prevent his wolf from taking over completely. The taste of his brother's blood was already thick on his tongue and he hadn't moved yet.

Marcus gripped his shoulder and forced him to remain seated. His father came from the other side to wrap his fingers around his forearm exerting the authority of his alpha to calm him and his beast.

Stefan prudently removed his arms from around the women, careful to make no sudden moves. Never taking his eyes off Simon, he stepped away from Rose and slowly backed from the room.

Simon intently watched Stefan move away from Rose very slowly, the scent of rage he was emitting flooded the room. He barely suppressed a growl as Stefan put distance between himself and Rose. It took everything he had to remain in human form and not launch himself at the threat Stefan represented. His wolf snarled and snapped for release. Knowing he had to protect the shifter community and not expose himself to a human, and accomplishing it, were two different things. His jaw quivered from the pressure of his gritted teeth.

"Just breathe, everything's all right, just breathe. Simon, look at your hands. You need to take care of that," Isaac whispered quietly so only Simon would hear.

He breathed deeply, closed his eyes and centered himself, a practice he had perfected in the marines. That's when he caught a new scent, the first wisps of heavenly fragrance coming from Anna's friend. It was coffee and cinnamon rolls.

He thought he had smelled it earlier when Rose touched him but it had been so fleeting he assumed he'd imagined it.

Rose gave Anna a questioning look, *why was everyone acting so strange*? It was then she saw the brother called Simon was now sitting up on the couch.

Glancing around the room, everyone's face wore a shocked expression. All except Isaac and Emma. She saw them wink at each other as Simon stood, straightened his shirt and walked toward her.

"It's my pleasure to meet such a beautiful woman," he said as he took her soft, warm hand.

Everything inside him stilled except his heart, which hammered at his ribs at a staccato pace. Mesmerized, his breath caught in his throat and it felt as if the world stopped spinning. *Her eyes are incredible.* Brilliant blue, glistening with a bit of amusement still remaining from whatever Anna had just said to her. Soft, gentle, intelligent eyes. A man could lose his heart in those eyes... or find the other half of his soul. His attraction was met and matched by that of his wolf. The poor beast was desperate to rub against her, marking her as its own.

"Hello." Her voice was like a balm to his tortured soul, gentle, lovely. Sexy. A blend of preacher's daughter and sexy siren that had his wolf cocking its head with more than a little interest. "It's nice to meet you."

He had never reacted so forcefully to a voice before. It released something deep inside him that he hadn't even known had been imprisoned. It was like having a blindfold and earplugs removed to see and hear the world for the first time.

Simon closed his eyes and sighed. His chest expanded as he took a deep breath, slowly his smile grew a little larger and he opened his eyes. Her intense gaze sent such a zing to his soul, he didn't even notice the other people in the room.

"I look forward to spending time with you." Never taking his eyes from hers, he gave a gentle kiss to the back of her hand and inclined his head. Still clasping her hand, he straightened and walked backward as he led her to the couch.

Small gasps were heard all around the room that didn't seem to penetrate the fog that had taken up residence in his head.

He'd finally heard the voice in his mind that he'd been longing for—Rose's voice. He had heard her startled surprise when Stephan had snuck up on her. Somehow, she had yanked him out of the darkness with her quiet presence. She hadn't needed to raise her voice or use any form of force to accomplish this miracle.

He took the opportunity to admire her as they sat quietly together. Out of reflex he cocked his head to the left like a dog. *I've spent way too much time as a wolf.* Silently he studied her, average height—not tall, but not exceedingly short. *Holy Moses, her body is a feast waiting to happen*, a luscious woman's figure. A body that even Jane Russell would envy. His fingertips tingled, she was all supple sumptuous curves, crying out for his caress.

Glancing back at him, she didn't maintain eye-to-eye contact. His blatant attention seemed to make her uncomfortable. She was a bombshell, but from her rosy pink cheeks, he was sure she didn't realize it. There was no rancid scent of arrogance to this woman. What he did smell was the scent from a humble, shy person. More importantly, he smelled the delicious fragrance of coffee and cinnamon rolls. The scent was utterly intoxicating, and his wolf wanted to roll in it.

Still holding her hand he leaned closer. "Take a walk with me?"

Her eyes grew wide. Uncertain what to do, she looked to Anna. Her friend gave her a small nod and when she frowned Anna nodded more adamantly. "Um…okay."

Without so much as a glance to the others, they walked out the door. Unsure what to say, they strolled in silence. A warm, moist breeze caressed their skin as they neared the river, it caused her hair to flutter on her cheeks. The sight made his fingers itch to feel the silken strands. He stopped midway in his reach to brush them from her face. "May I?"

Her shy smile and deep blush were his answer as he tucked the flyaway ends behind her delicate ear. The tiny contact had his groin swelling beyond the capacity of his jeans. *The walk back could prove to be both heaven and hell,* he thought.

As she stood with her back to him taking in the beauty of the sunset on the water, she shivered slightly in the cooler river breeze. "Here, Rose, let me warm you." She stiffened as he drew her back to his warm, hard chest. To her utter mortification, her body of its own accord molded itself to his chest and hips like two pieces of a puzzle snapping into place. Stupid body!

His wolf wanted to howl at the feel of her curves firmly against his hard form.

He noted as he held her that she was the perfect height for him to see over the top of her head. His nostrils flared, being so close to her scent. Her hair was drenched in it. Like a dog rolling in a fresh cut lawn, he had to rub his chin through the spun silk. Covering himself in the delicate perfume made just for him. They stood quietly wrapped in each other's embrace as the sun bid them goodnight "We should head back," he said as he pressed his lips to her hair in a chaste kiss.

Nodding in agreement, she drew away, taking her warmth with her.

He sucked in his breath as she turned to walk back to the house. Rose had the fresh-faced girl next-door beauty he preferred. She was the sweet, soft-spoken blonde, who always ended up being the popular girl's best friend but never the popular one herself. To Simon she was the homecoming queen and Miss Louisiana rolled into one. Her skin looked so soft he had to run his finger down her cheek to see if it was as soft as it looked. It was.

Chapter 5

BBQ

Isaac and Emma hugged Anna and Cade goodnight and thanked her for hosting Thanksgiving. Like most parties, the initiation of one person leaving caused a domino effect, Marcus and Stefan followed suit. That left Simon with no choice but to leave as well.

"Thank you for the fantastic dinner, Anna." He shook Cade's hand before turning to Rose. Raising her hand to his lips. "I'm so glad you came for a visit. I sincerely hope I can see more of you while you're here." Before he lost his nerve, he walked out the door.

His wolf fought to remain with its mate and his newly recovered but iffy control almost slipped before he was out of sight. *I may be back, but this is going to take some effort to remain human.* The further he moved from Rose the harder it became to maintain his form. He rushed into his house before he shifted and ended up sleeping outside for the night.

Anna knocked on Rose's door, she knew her friend was still confused by her reaction to Simon.

"Come in," muffled from the room.

"I thought I'd check on you now that everyone has gone home."

Rose smoothed the quilt on the bed. "I don't know

49

what I was thinking? I walked up to a total stranger and started touching him, I wanted to pet him for cryin' out loud! And I felt like I had a right to do it. Like I own him or something."

"It sounds like you are having the same attraction to Simon as I have to Cade. To be honest, it's not a bad thing." She grinned at her friend.

"He scares the crap out of me and yet I can't stay way from him. I feel like I have another person inside me, walking me around like a marionette. I wish Jack and Michael were here," she said sadly.

"What would you do if they were here? They can't protect you from yourself, you goof."

"I don't know, they always take care of me and I automatically turn to them. They're my family," she whispered.

"I know, baby. Don't be so scared. What you just experienced is the draw of a Le Beau. Of course I don't think you'll have the same reaction to all of them. You didn't react that way with Marcus or Stefan right?"

"No." Rose shook her head as she recalled meeting the other men.

"Then I think you and Simon have a strong attraction to each other and you should enjoy it."

"Are you nuts! I'm not going to make a fool of myself. He's way out of my league."

"I promise you, Simon is not out of your league and he's VERY interested in you. He was devouring you with his eyes and he was so charming, the way he took you for a stroll."

Rose smiled and nibbled her fingernail. "He was, wasn't he?" Her eyes shined.

"And for the record, I've always considered you a strong woman who can protect herself. You're the only one who doesn't see it. You have sweet dreams and I'll see you in the morning." Anna hugged her and said goodnight.

Yawning, Simon stretched his tired and achy muscles, sleeping with his mate several acres away and under a different roof had been both heaven and hell. He let out a disgusted chuff, *what sleep?* Sleep was not going to be his friend for a while. *Man she's hot!* Rose's innocence and vulnerability had caught him in her unintentional web. He'd been a prisoner there ever since.

Closing his eyes he shifted to human and scrubbed his fingers through his hair as he warred with himself. *God, I'm such a mess.* His instincts demanded he claim his mate, but his mental and physical issues made him doubt if he should.

Yawning again, he was exhausted. He waffled on the subject all night, the light of day hadn't brought answers either. With no solution forthcoming, he gave it a rest and headed for the shower to wash the cobwebs from his brain.

He groaned in frustration as he visualized Rose, her blue eyes filled with concern, blond tendrils of glossy hair framed a lovely face, and her curvy body moved gracefully as she followed him to the shower…no couch, she moved to the couch. Obviously, the shower wasn't his friend either.

As he was gaining control of his wayward

thoughts, Rose unwittingly broke through on their telepathic link. She was imagining him in the shower, dammit, he groaned. This was torture.

His cock stood at attention, rock-hard and ready every time he thought of her, he was so screwed.

With no other option presenting itself, he took himself in hand. *God, I'm pathetic.* His inner argument from his endless sleepless night resurfaced. He'd examined his situation in detail. He was so damaged, he and Anna weren't sure he would ever be completely healed. He couldn't consider pursuing Rose while he was unsure how long he could hold human form before reverting to wolf. It was both unfair and dangerous to her. Humans weren't allowed knowledge of their existence unless they were mates or family and there were shifters who hunted any human who did. He would have to keep his distance until he made a final decision on the matter. *I should let her live a happy human life without my baggage. I won't let her down like I did Mark.*

Struggling to zip his overly tight jeans, he shoved his hands into his pockets and adjusted his position. Goddess, he had it bad. He reminded his unruly lower half, *I'm a damaged wolf, far from healed and I can't saddle Rose with that.*

How long would he moon over a woman he couldn't and wouldn't have?

Until she went back to Denver?

Until she married someone else?

He growled at the thought of another man putting his hands on Rose's delectable body. Simon fought the purely feral instinct that escalated at the thought of another man touching his mate.

He shook his head, trying to dispel the unacceptable images, surprised by his possessive reaction. He'd have to find a way to handle this and allow her to live her life. He had no right to deny her happiness because he had issues. *Yeah...I don't like this at all...it just sucks.* All he'd ever wanted was to find his mate and now that he had, he was denied his claim. He didn't know how to deal with his jealousy, but then he had never needed a woman like this before.

He had prided himself on his control but now he could think of little else but the pretty woman who had snagged his attention.

You're afraid of her.

Simon scowled at the thought. *Like hell I am!* He wasn't afraid of anything, and he definitely didn't fear Rose O'Leary. She just...was too good for a damaged wolf like him.

Rose lay in bed thinking about everything that had happened with Simon and her discussion with Anna. *He obviously has a very strong attraction to me and really doesn't like other men to touch me.* To be truthful, he was downright scary when other men tried to touch her. The fact was his possessiveness should've sent her running for the hills. *So why am I not running?*

Men didn't often give her the hot sultry gazes she received from Simon. Sure, they were very attentive once they got to know her and no longer looked at her as a dress size. She was the first to admit she was plump and she had accepted that a long time ago. It was the hot, skinny *puntas* who usually garnered the steamy looks like the ones Simon gave her. And she honestly didn't know what to do with them. *Anna said I'm strong and confident and Simon is attracted to me.* She smiled at herself in the mirror over her lowboy dresser. *You can do this. Just talk to him coherently if he tries to talk to you.*

Thinking of him had her imagining all kinds of naughty thoughts. Images of Simon naked, water sluicing over his chest and ...lower...

She made for the bathroom that was shared between her room and John's. Listening for her chance to shower, she heard the water stop and a door open. She grabbed her bathroom bag ready to take her turn. Imagining Simon was on the other side of the door dressing instead of John had her excited. She felt like she had a schoolgirl crush, complete with silly giggles.

Then she caught sight of herself in the mirror. Good lord! She leaned closer, she was scary pale. Her blue eyes were puffy with dark circles. She hated the death warmed over look she got when she didn't get enough sleep. She'd lain awake most of the night thinking about Simon. Wanting him. Fantasizing about him. She even swore she'd heard him in her head again. At one point she would have bet good money that she felt him touch her. *Ridiculous.*

She liked being in his company, A LOT. And she was curious to see what kind of sense of humor he had. She really liked the feel of his hands on her skin and his lips kissing her hand and hair. Water flowed over her body and she stood under the warm spray imagining his hands on her breasts. *Oh come on, admit it. There is nothing you don't like about him. Girl, you got it bad.*

She closed her eyes, smiling to herself. Imagining Simon was in the shower with her. Startled, she almost slipped when her groan echoed around the ceramic enclosure. With her forehead pressed against the shower tile she sighed, *Please let him feel the same way.* Her last boyfriend left her heart shattered in a million pieces. That had been over a year ago. She was very skittish about letting herself fall too hard for another pretty boy. That never ended well for her. Breathing a curse, she was too late, that train had already left the station and she was in deep.

"I'm not going to let the past dictate my future," she recited to herself ten times. Her shrink had told her whenever she fell back into the roll of a victim or let her past control her she needed to recite her mantra.

Drying her hair, she scowled at her reflection. There was nothing to do but apply extra makeup to cover the dark circles under her eyes to make her look a little less corpse like. Then enjoy the day with Anna, Cade, and maybe Simon.

Fifteen minutes later she emerged from the bathroom dressed and pleased with her appearance. This day was going to be great.

The wonderful aromas of coffee and breakfast drew her to the kitchen. "Good morning," she said as Cade and Anna came into view.

"Would you like some coffee?" Cade asked, raising his cup for a sip.

"I'd love some. Thank you."

He rose to grab her a mug. "Black or doctored?"

"Cream and sugar, please."

He handed it to her, handle forward, so she wouldn't have to touch the hot body of the cup. "Isaac called, he wants to host a barbecue for John, Thomas, and you," Cade announced.

"He has invited a few friends as well. Since the boys are able to stay a few more days, he grabbed the chance to have a cook-out. That man will use any excuse he can. Much like how the French Quarter seizes any reason for a parade." Anna laughed. "I hope that's all right with you."

"I'm okay with whatever you plan. I have all the time in the world. Who are the friends he invited?" She sipped the coffee and looked at Anna over the rim.

"Some of the local guys. He wanted to introduce the boys to a few men their age. Anna is hoping if they make friends they will want to move here," Cade said and winked at his mate.

"That's awfully nice of him, it sounds like fun."

"I need a few things from the store, you want to run errands with me?" Anna asked Rose. "We should be back in a few hours."

"Perfect, I noticed a few things I forgot to pack this morning and I can pick them up while we're out."

Walking the aisles in the tiny corner store, Rose felt apprehensive… the hair stood on the back of her neck. It was like someone was watching her.

Intently.

Menacingly.

Turning her head, she scanned the aisle, looking

for the source of her discomfort. But no one was there.

Every time she checked, her aisle was empty. Strange. Standing before a small mirror, she picked up a pair of sunglasses. As she lifted them to her face, she glimpsed a man in the reflection glaring at her. Her breath hitched as she spun around. No one. Glancing left and right, she was alone. Heart hammering, she grabbed a random pair of glasses and hurried to Anna.

"Are you okay, you're shaking?" Anna looked her over, a little worried.

"Let's pay, we can talk in the car," she whispered.

Anna searched her face again. "All right, if you have everything, I'm ready to check out."

Minutes later they were on the road for home. "Okay, spill," Anna demanded.

"A man was watching me in the store. I think he was following me around, I spotted him once but he moved so fast I lost track of him."

Anna's eyes flew to hers, alarm spread across her face. "Can you describe him? We need to tell Cade as soon as we get home."

"No, I barely got a glimpse of him. Do I need to be concerned?"

Looking a little guilty Anna confessed to Rose her experience with the mob boss and his goons. "It could be them looking for payback. Cade and the boys will want to put bodyguards on us when we leave the property from now on."

"You, live a scary life, my friend."

"It's not so bad, really." Anna brushed it off, she didn't want Rose to worry during her visit. The rest of the ride home they discussed the barbeque and avoided the scary events of the shopping trip.

Isaac rubbed his hands together like a mad scientist, he had a party to plan. Anna's sons expressing an interest in meeting some of the local guys was a perfect excuse. Not only would he get to do one of his favorite past times, but he also got to prod his son with a few unsuspecting suitors for Rose.

Last night, after Simon's initial reaction to meeting his mate, Isaac had sensed his son's doubt and anxiety throughout the night. If Simon thought he could walk away from her, he had another thing coming. His plan to put a few single shifter males in close proximity to Rose should get Simon back on track.

He tapped his chin, *who will tweak Simons nerves the most?* He barked out a laugh, *Tony and Sam!* He grabbed his cell phone and dialed the young men.

"Hello?"

"Hello, Tony, this is Isaac."

"Your highness, what can I do for you?"

"Tony, you know how I feel about you calling me that," he growled.

"Sorry, Sir, I have a hard time not seeing you as my king."

"Forget about it, I'm having a small barbeque at my house tonight. Anna's sons are in town and her single friend Rose is staying with us."

"Really? A single friend of Anna's? I'm in." He could practically hear the man salivating.

"The party starts at 7 p.m."

"I will try to be there at seven but I may be late."

Simon: Le Beau Brothers

"That's fine, I'll have extra food in case you make it for dinner. We'll see you when you get here."

One down, one to go, this is just too much fun. He was humming to himself as he dialed Sam and repeated the invite.

Christ, what am I a thirteen-year-old girl? Simon stood naked in front of his closet. *How can I have all these clothes and nothing to wear?* The party started at seven and he intended be there before any of the other men invited arrived. He wanted to assess the enemy the moment they stepped from their cars.

He pulled a shirt from its hanger, scowled, and tossed it to the floor. There were ten shirts scattered across the room before one met with approval. *Halfway there*, he thought as he turned his search to pants. Once dressed, he noticed the destruction called his bedroom. *Good thing Stefan can't see this.*

Simon made an extra effort in the grooming department, he couldn't remember ever shaving a second time. He wanted his face baby smooth. Rose would be there tonight, just the thought of seeing her again had his wolf salivating. *No.. No.. No, you need to let her go,* he reminded himself. *If I keep doing one eighties on this I'm going to give myself whiplash. Stupid wolf needs to let her go.*

Scanning the deck, he grabbed an Adirondack chair and positioned it close to the stairs, satisfied with a perfect view of both the patio doors as well as the driveway. There was no way for Rose to join the party without his knowing, and he could see the enemy coming.

Simon tried to draw air into his lungs, but there didn't seem to be an adequate supply. Rose trailed behind Anna and Cade as their group came up the stairs. Her head slowly turned as if she sensed him. Their eyes locked, vaguely he thought, *the cliché is true, time can stand still*. For that moment they were the only people on the deck, no one else existed in the world.

He held very still as her gaze tentatively began moving very slowly over him, taking in the fine sheen of sweat coating his skin and whatever else a woman notices in a man. When her gaze returned to his eyes she seared him to his very core. He worried she could see beyond the outer facade he presented to the world to the tormented soul within. At once, the chatter receded from the party and all he heard was her, in his mind as she said *Simon Le Beau, you are a most intriguing man. If I had half a brain I'd be packing for Denver right now.* The pain from having too many people close by evaporated and his old control returned.

He remained very still, afraid if he moved the pain would come slamming back. He watched Rose moving through the party speaking first to Emma and then Cade. As she moved further from him the pain began to build, if she moved closer it subsided. This was interesting; her soothing balm seemed to have a distance restriction.

She neared Marcus, and instantly his wolf went on alert. He'd never been a jealous man and yet, feeling the astonishing flood of jealousy shocked him. No, not just jealousy, but that plus protectiveness and ownership. Shoving his hands into his pockets, he'd never experienced this emotion, and he didn't like it, not at all.

You could have knocked him over with a feather. He sat for what felt like five minutes with his mouth hanging open before the realization sunk in. He may not be able to walk away from her like he had intended.

His pain was receding and he was having no problem maintaining his form, thanks to Rose. Did she feel this attraction between them too? He hoped so. He sensed she desired him but did she have affection for him? He prayed he wasn't alone in his need of her. *I should give this another day or two. I can't have my abilities fail me when Rose is involved.*

As their eyes locked again and soft emotions filled her gaze he received his answer.

He could almost feel the softness of her skin, taste her lips. She was his beacon in the night. He was trapped in a web of sensual and emotional need. It took enormous effort to hold small talk with the family when his wolf wanted to carry her off where they could be alone.

He found, over and over through the night, regardless of his good intentions, all he could do was stare. He was spellbound by this woman, his woman. He focused on the soft strands of her golden blond hair begging to be touched. It was so great to have his wolf senses working correctly again. Her skin gleamed, impossibly soft and inviting. Her neck begged for his kisses and his mark. It was tan and a long expanse of skin was bared whenever she turned her head. It was screaming for his attentions and driving him to the brink of insanity. All he could think about was pressing his mouth there and wandering, exploring, losing himself in the lushness of her body.

Dinner had long ago been eaten yet the party wore on as he struggled to control his wolf's demands in front of his friends and family. His jeans were so tight, he was afraid he'd burst, his aching, throbbing body had hardened to the point that the denim had him in a strangle hold. This party had better end early or he would have blue balls for a week. *Think Simon, think. How can you get her alone? STOP THAT! You can't do that to her unless you can control your shift.* Grimacing at himself, *just call me Sybil with these multiple personalities.*

Rose sucked in her breath, what the heck was going on? She would swear she just heard Simon speaking in her head. Trying to be nonchalant, she looked at him out of the corner of her eye. Simon was fixated on her in an almost animalistic way. It was a bit scary and exciting at the same time.

"Hello, I'm Tony," pulled her from her thoughts, Rose looked into a pair of eyes so dark they were almost black as she accepted his outstretched hand.

"Hello, I'm Anna's friend, Rose."

"I'm pleased to meet you, Anna's friend Rose. If I had known such a beautiful single woman would be here, I would have arrived much earlier."

She felt the heat rise to her face at his comment. Before she could recover another man reached for her hand.

"Hello, beauty. I'm Sam." He playfully pushed Tony to the side before he bent to kiss her hand. His lips never had a chance of making contact.

An animalistic snarl emanated behind her. Startled she looked over her shoulder as both men backed away, Simon stood casually leaning on the railing with his legs stretched out in front of him. *What the heck?* She search again but there wasn't a dog in sight.

When she turned back to speak to Tony and Sam, they were both across the deck. *Okay...?*

Watching unmated males touch his mate had been too much, his wolf hung at the surface and he knew, this time, his wolf would win out. Knowing his pain would return, he had no choice but to leave before he shifted in front of Rose. The moment she looked away he stole down the stairs and into the night. He would take a run while he gathered his control. This reaction and complete lack of control answered the question he had struggled with all night. He wasn't fit to be her mate.

Two hours later, he entered his home and caught the scent of his father. He had wondered if he would get a visit after leaving suddenly.

"Hello, Father," he said as he entered the living room.

"Are you all right, Simon?" Concern laced his father's voice. His eyes followed him as he crossed the room.

"I'm better now, the run helped," he said as he flopped onto the couch like a teenager.

"What happened? One minute you were there and the next you disappeared."

He scrubbed his face, sighed, and sat a little straighter before he met his father's gaze. "I've met my mate, it's Rose."

"That's wonderful!" His face lit up before it crashed into a scowl. "But why is that a problem?"

"Come on, Dad, be real. I'm damaged. Tonight when the males touched her I almost shifted right there on the deck. I can't be a proper mate to her. It's enough to ask a human female to accept a shifter, but it's too much to ask her to tie herself to a broken one."

Isaac moved to sit next to Simon. "I don't have answers for you or your problem. I've never dealt with this before. Life would be so easy if we had all the answers, wouldn't it? Will you ever have complete control over your wolf again? Will Rose agree to be your mate? Will you ever be the man you were?"

Simon went cold at his words. "I don't need to be reminded of my issues, Dad. I know them better than anyone... intimately. So, what do you suggest I do?"

He didn't answer immediately. "I know from personal experience, humans are amazing in their capacity to adapt and give love freely. Don't sell Rose short because you're afraid of what might or might not happen. Instead, maybe you should focus on recuperating as best you can. If you need a push to keep moving forward in your recovery and courtship, just think about what will happen if you don't give your mating a chance."

Quietly he whispered, "Would she be happy without me....with a human?" He wasn't sure he wanted to know the answer.

Isaac shrugged. "Maybe, maybe not. Life is a

gamble, Simon. Who's to say? Maybe there's a human who could love her. But will he ever love her as much as you do?"

"What should I do?" His shoulders slumped a bit.

"I think you already know."

Simon knew deep in his heart, she was a priceless gift. He had only one mate and would never get another. He sat in silence as he thought over what his father said.

Isaac stood to leave then paused. "All you can do is give it your best shot and trust that Rose is the woman I believe her to be. A free thinker, who ignores mainstream pressures and goes her own way. She's stronger and more willing than you give her credit for. So what will you choose to do? Fight for your mate or give up and leave her to try to find happiness with a human? I'm sorry I don't have an easy answer for you." He clapped Simon on the shoulder and left the house.

Isaac's question hung in Simon's mind as he stewed over the conversation. He didn't know what choice to make and his father hadn't really helped. His lips pulled back in a silent snarl as the image of Rose naked in another man's arms loomed in his mind. Claws emerged at the ends of his fingers and he knew without a shadow of a doubt, he would never be a strong enough man to let her go. Any male touching her in other than a respectful or brotherly manner would meet a bloody end.

Maybe his father helped more than he realized. That man knew just the right buttons to push to get the response he desired.

Both his wolf's soul and the man thanked the Goddess for this woman. She was a gift more precious than he deserved, and he was honored he'd been blessed with her as his mate. He vowed to work harder than ever before to be the man he once was. The man who had joined the Marines four years prior to serve his country. The man who had been brave and strong, but also loving, tender, and filled with hope. She deserved that man and he was going to give him to her.

With renewed resolve and determination he decided to find Anna first thing in the morning, then he would locate Rose.

Chapter 6

Recovery for Rose

The next morning, he found Anna in her kitchen, blurry eyed, with the largest coffee mug he'd ever seen. "Should you be drinking coffee?" He was sure he'd heard somewhere that pregnant women shouldn't have caffeine.

"It's decaf. I'm pretending to drink the real stuff, hoping to trick my body into waking up." She grinned. "What brings you over so bright and early?"

"I'd like to know if we could speed up the healing process. As you may have guessed, Rose is my mate. I can't pursue her until I have control over my shifting."

She sipped her coffee and studied him for a moment. "Why do you feel you need to be in more control in order to pursue her?"

He ran his fingers through his hair in frustration. "I almost lost control last night at the party and I would have shifted in front of her. I can't have that happen until she's ready to accept it."

She quietly nodded and tapped the side of her cup, thinking through his request. "Your mother taught me a few new things we can try. We've been concentrating on ways to help you, I'm confident what I have in mind will work."

"I'm ready for anything you want to try." He leaned closer in his excitement. "When can we start?"

She snatched a lock of hair from his head.

"What the hell, Anna!"

"I need some of your hair for one of the items," she said as if people pull out other people's hair every day. Then she made a list of things she would need. "I need to go shopping in the Quarter. While I'm doing that, you can prepare your home with powerful healing colors. Your mother has many items to take care of that."

He wasn't sure where she was going with all this, but she was an extremely powerful healer and if she believed this would work, it would.

"Start by adding these colors throughout your house; red, which enhances power and strength. It will help you fight for control. And blue to bring tranquility to the soul and promote healing of the body and self. Plus, add in gold for strengthening the mind."

"I have those colors in a few items. Do I need to put them anywhere special?"

"Put them in plain sight and in an arrangement to surround you. If you have clothing in those colors, wear them. I'll gather the herbs, crystals, and candles. While we are busy doing our jobs, I'll have your mother make a putsi pouch and a magical poppet. You'll wear the putsi around your neck until I tell you to remove it."

"Thank you, little sister, this means so much to me."

She hugged him. "Believe me, I know exactly what this means to you."

She waited for Simon to leave and then woke Rose. Anna knocked on her bedroom door. "Rose, are you awake? Would you like to go to the French Quarter with me this morning?"

She heard sheets rustling and Rose yawning. "Sure, give me a few minutes to get ready."

Anna told Cade her plan to shop in the French Quarter for healing supplies. He had told her he didn't want them to leave the plantation unprotected. Cade agreed to let them go without escort as long as he could notify Etienne and have him watch over them once they arrived.

Faster than Anna thought possible they were driving to town. Rose normally took forever to get ready. She had her nose buried in a cup of coffee, the real stuff, as she tried to shake off the cobwebs.

"I need to buy a few things at some specialty shops, is there anything you want to look for?"

"I heard there are interesting bargains at the French Market. I'd like to check that out and see what they have."

The ride to New Orleans was quiet as Rose sipped her coffee and enjoyed the scenery. Before she knew it, they were parking.

"How about we each do our shopping then meet back at the car to stow any purchases. Once we're done I want to take you to meet my friend Richie and get lunch."

"Sure, sounds like a plan," she said as she pulled her purse onto her shoulder.

Rose meandered toward the market on the east end of French Market Place. After two hours of browsing she had found a few treasures to purchase and was heading back toward the car. She walked a block up Barracks Street and turned on Decatur to meet Anna where she had parked. She slowed as she felt the sensation of someone watching her, it was the same sensation she felt at the corner store. The crowd had thinned dramatically, leaving her feeling exposed and vulnerable.

Checking her surroundings, she half-expected to find the man from the reflection, not that she'd seen him well enough to recognize him. She shook the chill off and was laughing at herself when rough hands grabbed her from behind. It happened so fast she couldn't scream for help before she was pulled into an abandoned retail space.

The grip holding her eased as her assailant shut them in from prying eyes. Taking advantage of her one chance at survival, she broke loose and tried for the exit praying for a still open door. What she found was a second man blocking her escape. He was a scruffy-looking man and eyed her with manic interest. Fear assaulted her. His attention was too focused to be sane. Way too intense and threatening, as he advanced on her.

"What do you want?" her voice barely a squeak.

His silent sneer was his reply.

"You didn't tell us she was a pretty little thing, Travis," a voice said behind her.

She spun around, alarmed there was a third man, this one with dark hair she hadn't known was there. She glanced about, frantic for a weapon, a pipe lay near her feet. It wasn't her first choice but beggars couldn't be choosers and she wouldn't go without a fight.

Dark Hair lunged for her as she swung the pipe with wicked accuracy.

Snarling he held his busted arm for a moment before he punched her hard. "Don't fight me, bitch!"

Her head snapped back and blood trickled from her nose, the impact sent her stumbling. She was so scared, she reacted totally on instinct. She righted herself and kneed him hard. "Bastard!"

Scruffy snarled at Dark Hair. "Don't hit her asshole, she's mine."

"Since when?" Blondie barked.

Shit, there are too many of them.

As Dark Hair doubled over she dashed past him for the door. She rattled it in desperation, locked with a security grate over the glass. Her already hammering heart, raced faster, she was trapped. "HELP! Someone help me!"

Blondie grabbed her shoulder and spun her around, tearing her shirt in the process.

Lust filled his eyes. "No one is going to help you. We'd only planned to deliver you, but I don't think they'll mind if we play with you first."

With an ear splitting screech, the metal grate ripped from its brackets and the door crashed open. Blondie was hurtled to the floor.

Her terrified gaze shot to the newcomer and she wanted to cry in relief until she saw his expression. He was scarier than Scruffy, Blondie, and Dark Hair combined. He was commanding. Intense. And good lord, he was really handsome. There was a savage gleam in his eyes that was alarming as he put himself between her and her attackers. He looked as if he could easily kill a person and not think twice.

She staggered back and watched in awe as her unknown McHottie fought with incredible skill.

"This ain't your business, vampire," Dark Hair growled and flashed something shiny. He came at her hero with a knife in his good hand.

Blondie grabbed McHottie's right arm and Scruffy latched onto his left. Dark Hair got one good slash across McHottie's chest before he smashed Dark Hair between Blondie and Scruffy like a sandwich.

All three stumbled back and then regrouped in a circle around her and McHottie.

"You are in my territory, mutts. Everything here is my business." He caught Dark Hair's wrist and twisted until the knife fell from his hand. Then he backhanded him so hard, Dark Hair rebounded off the wall. A cloud of dust billowed around her.

Scruffy snatched her arms behind her so she could hardly move.

As she stood immobilized Blondie circled McHottie looking for an opening. With newfound bravado that only having a hero with you brings, her self-defense training kicked in and she drew forward as far as she could then slammed her head back into Scruffy. A loud crack sounded close to her ear. *Yes! I must have cracked a rib.* He released her and she spun, planted her feet shoulder width apart and swung her pipe at Scruffy's head with all her might. With a loud crack she made a direct hit and watched as he collapsed, down for the count.

Blondie threw himself at McHottie. They went to the floor in a thick cloud of dust. Between the lack of light and the cloud in the air, Rose could hardly see the men only a few feet from her. Growling and hissing came from the ball of flying arms and legs. She didn't dare smack one of them with her pipe because odds were good she would hit McHottie.

A dark dirt covered figure rose from the floor and snatched the other around the back of his neck, lifted the body over his head and slammed it to the floor.

Rose screamed and stumbled back until the wall ended her retreat.

"Are you okay?" A very bloody and dirty McHottie asked Rose. "Did he hurt you?"

Before she could answer, Dark Hair attacked McHottie again from behind. *What is this guy, the terminator?* Dark Hair hit her hero full force, but he didn't so much as teeter or flinch. Dark Hair had a length of silver chain and wrapped it around McHottie's neck and shoulders.

Enraged, McHottie grabbed Dark Hair's arm and flipped him into the wall so hard a crack formed.

He slid to the ground, and must have had enough as he scurried out the door.

McHottie hissed at Scruffy and grabbed him. "Get out of my town or die." He threw him out the door, all the way to the center of the street.

Finally McHottie snatched the limp body of Blondie and tossed him next to Scruffy.

Her sexy hero turned to her again. "Did he hurt you?"

"Just a bloody nose, are you okay? Are you bleeding or is that Blondie's blood?"

"Blondie?"

"The blond guy you wrestled with on the floor."

Etienne chuckled. "Oh. No, I am fine. It is his blood."

Relieved to be alive, she was shaking so badly she wasn't even sure how her legs continued to hold her upright.

Seconds later McHottie sagged to the floor.

Kneeling next to him she was a bit confused, he just told her he wasn't injured. Then she looked closer at the chain wrapped around his neck and shoulder. "Why did he wrap you in chains, and why is your skin smoking where it's touching you?"

"If you would please remove the chains, I will be happy to tell you."

A shiver ran up her spine, this wasn't normal. "I don't think so. Explain first and then I'll think about it." She had just gotten away from a gang of rapists she wasn't going to trust another stranger simply because he was polite.

Sighing, he said, "I am a vampire."

Falling on her butt, she crab walked away from him until the wall stopped her retreat.

"I am sorry, I did not mean to frighten you. I am normally not so abrupt but as you can see I am having a very bad day." Lifting his nose he took a long sniff in her direction. "You know the Le Beaus." A smile broke across his face. "And…" He cocked his head to the side. "My good friends Jack and Michael from Denver."

"Ye..Ye…Yes," she stuttered.

"Cade is a very good friend of mine. How is his lovely wife Anna?" he wheezed.

Refusing to go near him, she asked, "You know

Anna? And wait a minute, you don't mean my foster brothers, Jack and Michael?"

"Yes, I do mean your brothers. I met Anna a few months ago. I hear congratulations are in order, they have a baby on the way."

Keeping a close eye on him she dug her cell phone from her bag.

Anna answered, "Hi, Rose, are you finished shopping?"

"Not exactly, I need you to come to me on Decatur ASAP. I'm a half block short of Governor Nicholls Street."

"Are you okay? You don't sound right."

"Not really, I was mugged and the man who saved me says he knows you and my brothers. I'll watch for you on the sidewalk."

"I'm only three blocks away, are you hurt? Did you call 911?"

"Not yet, Anna, please just hurry." She could hear Anna running.

"I'm coming as fast as I can."

Rose turned back to the vampire. "If you really do know Anna and she says you're okay, I'll get those off you. She'll be here any second."

He gave her a pained but regal nod. Anger darkened his eyes as he glanced to her torn shirt. "The Le Beaus and your family will not take their treatment of you well."

Never taking her eyes off him, Rose barely made it back to the sidewalk before Anna ran up. "What happened? Oh my God, you're bleeding!"

"I was grabbed from behind and got punched

trying to get away. A man came to my rescue but I think he might be insane."

Eyeing her friend with concern Anna stepped through the destroyed door and gasped. "Etienne, what the heck happened here?"

Rose put her hand on Anna's arm. "You know him?"

She looked at Rose. "Yes, he's Cade's friend." She turned back to him. "Etienne, why are you on the floor?"

Before he could answer Rose added, "He said he's a vampire."

"Of course he is." She waved off Rose and knelt next to him examining the chains trying to decide how best to remove them.

"What the hell, Anna! You believe vampires are real!" She got down next to Anna, ready to protect her.

Gently taking Rose's face in her hands. "Sweetie, I'm so sorry to drag you into my insane world, but yes they are very real." She saw Rose wasn't buying it. "Okay, I get it. I'd need proof too. Believe me they are very real. But, don't be afraid of him, he's a very good friend." She turned to him and asked, "Etienne, may I ask you to show her your fangs?"

Without hesitation fangs appeared at the edges of Etienne's sexy full lips.

Rose grabbed Anna and tried to drag her toward the door. Patting her hand, Anna said, "I'll explain this, I promise. He won't hurt us. Do you trust me?" Her eyes searched Rose's face.

"You're absolutely sure about this, Anna? He could be a crazy person who files his teeth."

"I guarantee you, Etienne is real and would protect us with his life. He would never hurt us."

Rose looked between her friend and the man who rescued her. He hadn't hurt her when he could have and he risked himself to help her. Rose began to pace the dingy room and grumbled to herself. "Anna says she knows this guy and he won't hurt us….do I trust that? No. But I believe Anna…hmmmmmm, maybe give him a chance but stay prepared to knock him the hell out. Those teeth are coming nowhere near either of us!" She hefted her pipe as if testing its weight and balance. *Yeah, I can do that.*

"I'll give him a chance, but only because you know him." Then she looked him directly in the eye and pointed her pipe at his mouth. "But if he gets too close with those choppers, I'm whacking him with my pipe."

Anna looked horrified and shook her head. "I have so much to explain to you."

Rose joined Anna next to Etienne again and helped unwrapped the chains, cringing as her shaking hands caused the chain to touch virgin flesh and sizzle.

It had burned its way into his skin and left an angry looking wound.

He moaned in relief as his burns instantly healed. "Thank you."

"You're welcome," Rose said hesitantly.

"Anytime. And thank you for protecting Rose," Anna said.

He sat for a moment recovering, then stood to help the ladies from the floor. Rose hesitated to take his hand. "Please, allow me."

She placed her trembling hand in his and accepted his gallant assistance.

"That was either very brave or very stupid, jumping into the fight with a pipe," he said with a slight reprimand in his tone.

"You fought someone with a pipe?" Anna's voice went up a few octaves.

Scoffing, "I grew up in a very rough neighborhood and I've taken a lot of self defense classes. Believe me, I've dealt with worse than this." She glanced to the vampire, "So, Etienne, is it?" she asked as she wiped her hands clean.

"Etienne Delacour." He gave her a regal bow. "I am in your debt."

"I'm Rose O'Leary." She offered her name as she began to feel less skittish around him. "I think it's more like, I'm in your debt. So….silver, huh?"

"I know who you are, little Rose. I would appreciate it if you didn't share that information with anyone. We don't like for our weakness to be public knowledge."

"What do you mean you know who I am?"

"Twenty six years ago your brothers came to me for help with a lecherous, filthy man who had hurt you in unspeakable ways. They knew a few of my men from the streets and asked to speak with me. I was happy to rid the world of such a foul human. After that Jack and Michael remained in touch with my people and when they were old enough I partnered with them in their construction business."

Rose stared at him then slowly sank to the floor. She needed a moment to absorb what he'd confessed.

"Hun, are you okay?" Anna brushed Rose's hair from her face.

"I always wondered what happened to that bastard. For years, I expected him to show up and haul me back to his horrible shack of a house." Rose sat quietly for a minute, then she took a deep breath. "Thank you, Etienne. I owe you more than I can ever repay."

"You owe me nothing, but I would like to count you among my friends."

"I would be honored to be your friend and your secret is safe with us, but I think those other guys know something too," she teased. A sure sign she was becoming more comfortable.

"Not to worry, I will find them and deal with the problem," he said as he brushed his pants off.

"Well, thank you, Etienne, You really did save my life. So you are the silent partner my brothers are in business with?"

"Yes, they are very bright, talented young men. I have tutored them in the finer points of business and they flourished. I wish I could get them to relocate here. My fair city needs their talent to recover from the hurricane."

"I'll talk to them about it the next time I call them. Um, Etienne, do they know you are a vampire?"

Shaking his head he laughed. "Yes, they do. You are a pleasure, Rose, a unique human. I am glad we are finally friends. I watched you grow into a beautiful young woman and take on the business world in your own way. I always wanted to meet you."

"I'm glad too and I'll take that as a compliment,"

she said as she grinned at Anna's gaping expression.

"That is the first time I've heard you laugh, Et. It sounds good on you." Anna smiled. "Is there anything I should tell Cade about her attacker or was it a horrible coincidence?" Anna's voice was filled with concern.

"I will call him, and no, it was not a coincidence. Will you be remaining in the Quarter or going home?"

"Rose? Do you want to go home or would you like a stiff drink to calm your nerves."

"I'll take the drink, but I'd rather have it in the safety of your home."

Etienne stepped forward. "I do not trust that man to not return and try again. I will have one of my people follow you home."

"Thank you, I'm grateful for all your help and concern," Anna said as she hugged him and motioned for Rose to precede her out the door.

Rose plucked at the ripped shoulder seam of her blouse. "This was my favorite shirt." She scowled.

"I think we should get to the car as quickly as possible, before someone sees you and calls 911."

Finally belted inside the safety of the car, Anna looked Rose in the eye. "I'll tell you what little I know." She put the car in drive and headed for home.

"I met Etienne when I was dating Cade. He had something to do with keeping Tim away from me. I'm told a vampire can make you forget things and command you to do things. I'm not sure what that includes, but he commanded Tim to live in Las Vegas and never return to Louisiana. For that I'll be forever grateful."

"Is he the only one? He said he had men." Rose

leaned in closer, intrigued.

"No, there are more. I have no idea how many though. I about choked when you made the fang and pipe comment."

"Why, did I offend him?" She was horrified now that she thought back on it.

"Um…He's the king of the vampires and you threatened him with an old, rusty pipe."

"Shit!" Rose sat back in her seat and squeezed her eyes shut. "Can we call him or something so I can apologize?"

"Cade has his number if you want to call him."

She let out a huge breath. "Next time elbow me or something. Damn girl."

Anna glanced at her and busted out laughing at her appalled expression. "Can you tell Cade exactly what happened when we get home?"

"Is this about the mob again? Because those muggers are not part of a mob, they looked more like crazy homeless people."

"Etienne said it wasn't a coincidence, he knows something about your attackers that has him worried."

"Well, all right, if you think it's important."

"I do, New Orleans may have a reputation, but people don't get mugged in the Quarter in broad daylight the way you did."

"Now you have me worried, what would anyone want with me?"

"That's what we need to figure out."

"Etienne told the mugger he was in his territory, what did that mean?"

"He pretty much owns the French Quarter as far

as supes go. Unless you're his friend or associate, if you're a supe you need to announce yourself to him before you wonder around in the Quarter."

"Hold on, what's a supe?"

"Supernatural."

"So, you're telling me those men are vampires too!"

"Um….no…."

Rose's eyes grew huge before she scowled. "What are you not telling me?"

"There are other things around that aren't vampire."

"Like what! And how the hell do you know these things!" She was on the verge of a freak out.

"We're almost home. Can we talk about it there?"

She crossed her arms and huffed like a child. "Fine."

Moments later they collected their packages from the back seat. "I feel much better now that we're back. I'll happily avoid the French Quarter for a while."

"Well, I hope not. You'll be missing out on a wonderful time if you don't go for dinner and a night on Bourbon Street."

"Only with armed escort," she retorted.

As they passed through the great room, Cade asked, "How'd it go in town, did you find everything?"

"I found what I needed but Rose found more than she bargained for."

He shot up from his chair and snarled, "What happened."

"Rose, that's your cue."

She spent the next thirty minutes reliving the

entire nightmare for Cade as he scowled and became angrier by the minute. He seemed to breathe a sigh of relief when she told of her rescue by the vampire. *New Orleans is as freaky as people say it is,* she thought.

He looked at Anna. "He said he would call?"

"Yes, he wanted to discuss the situation and that it wasn't a coincidence."

He nodded. "If you need to leave the plantation for any reason, one of my brothers or I will join you. I don't want you ladies leaving without us again."

Rose raised her eyebrows at his command but remained silent. Before she could corner Anna and have her explain about the supes, Simon joined them.

Chapter 7

Anna's Magic

"Give me a minute to gather the last few things I need, Simon, and then I'll be right over." Saved from having to explain to Rose, she sped from the room.

Simon felt her tension the moment he neared her. Something was wrong. "Hello, Rose, how was your day?"

"Eventful," she quipped and walked from the room.

He felt her anger and hurt, what had he done to upset her? He was about to ask Cade when he noticed a disapproving look on his face. "What?"

"You. Are. An. Idiot."

"Hey now! I just walked through the door, I've hardly been here long enough to do anything stupid."

"Why did you abandon her last night at the party?"

So that's what this was about. "I barely got out of her sight before I lost control and shifted. I couldn't go furry in front of her, now could I?"

Cade rubbed his temples, "Sorry, mon frère, I had no idea. She was hurt and confused when you suddenly disappeared. Anna has told me things about her past and men. Tread lightly on her heart brother, she's fragile when it comes to relationships."

Simon took the chair next to his brother. "Shit, should I go talk to her? I never meant for her to be hurt by my issues. That is why they went to town today. Anna has new magic to try on me, I need to get my shifting under control before I can pursue Rose. I'm not safe around her the way I am. I can't fail her, Cade, if she were ever really hurt because of me, it would kill me."

"No. Let her be for now. She isn't going to be hurt because of you. Where do you get these ideas? What can I do to help?" He purposely didn't tell Simon about the muggers, he wanted his brother focused on healing. He and Etienne could handle whoever was stalking the women.

He shook his head. "No, just pray whatever she does to me today works. I better head home."

Cade clapped him on the back. "I have every faith in my mate. I'll keep Rose company while you're busy. Perhaps, mention what a catch you'll be." He winked.

"Yeah, try to soften her up for me. I don't like her upset." He glanced toward the hall she had gone down, and then walked out the door.

Simon paced his living room for an hour waiting for Anna when he heard voices. He opened the door to find her, his mother, and two other healers loaded with supplies.

He helped with their bags. "I wasn't expecting the entire healing team. Thank you all for coming."

Emma took charge. "Simon, you know Joan and Berti, right?"

"Yes, I've met them once or twice. It's nice to see you again, ladies."

"It's so nice to see you home, Simon," Berti replied.

"It's nice to see you too. How are you feeling?" Joan asked.

"Except for my shifting issue I'm perfect."

"Well, let's get on that," Emma said, ending the pleasantries. "It looks like you need more color around the house, this is a good start but more would be better. Anna, would you set him up with his bath while we decorate the house?"

"Absolutely, come on, Simon." She hustled out and left him to follow.

"Um...Anna...you're not going to watch me take a bath are you, because I like my head where it is."

"Of course I am, I have to be there to perform the ritual."

"Oh, hell no." He halted in the hallway short of the bathroom.

She laughed at his expression. "No, I'm kidding. I'll prepare the bath and then leave."

He smiled and blushed. "Good, because Cade is scary when you get him riled."

She chuckled and went to work on his bath. "This is a bath for illness, as the water fills the tub, I'll add white rose petals, white carnations, gardenias, and rosemary for healing. Then to cheer the soul, I add sliced orange, a half lemon, and neroli oil. Finally, to purify the soul, fresh coconut milk is added. All of these have already been blessed and prepared, once you get in, you need to imagine the heaviness in your heart and soul dissipating. Feel it rise from your body and float away leaving only lightness, happiness and love.

Simon: Le Beau Brothers

Remain in the bath until it begins to cool, then dress and rejoin us."

"That sounds easy enough." As soon as she closed the door, he stripped and lowered into the perfumed water. It felt so good, he had to suppress the moan rising from his chest. Closing his eyes he imagined the darkness and depression rising from him and drifting away. He imagined having complete control of his shifting and feeling in harmony with his wolf soul again. He thought about the events leading up to his squad leader's injury and pictured himself having not only control over his empathy but a sharper honed, improved ability to discern what he detects.

If pain had color or physical form, he was sure he would have seen it floating out of his body. His depression lifted and his guilt lessened. He would swear, if he got on a scale he would weigh fifty pounds less. The water was cooling and goose bumps started to rise. *Time for the next step.*

He returned to a room filled with candlelight and chanting. So as not to disturb them, he quietly sat in a chair. He noticed a low table had been set in the room with a satin cloth draped over it.

The room quieted and Anna opened her eyes, the power radiating from her was awe-inspiring. "Simon, please join me at the altar." She hung a small leather pouch around his neck. "This is a putsi, it has been filled with a piece of hematite, herbs, and an amulet. Wear it for three days and three nights. On the fourth day, hold it in your hand and visualize your goal of regaining complete control over your wolf and shifting."

She turned toward the altar and struck a match. "As I light the yellow candles and sprinkle the eucalyptus leaves, visualize yourself healthy and whole again. Then light the orange candle, then red candles on each side of the orange one. Watch the flames burn the illness away, and sense your strength returning to you. As you do that, repeat three times "I will no longer thirst on weakness and depression. My strength will help to heal me, and I will regain my health. Finally end with 'so shall it be' and snuff the candles out."

He scooted as close as he could on his knees and followed her instructions with only minor prompting. He was saying the spell for the third time when a surge of power rushed into his body. "So shall it be." And he blew out the candle. Startled he stared at Anna then his mother. "It feels like I was filled up and then someone stuck a stopper in me. And, the pain is gone too." He laughed, feeling truly joyful for the first time in years.

The ladies smiled and laughed with him. "That means it worked," Emma said as she patted his arm.

Next Anna brought forth a poppet made of muslin and filled with hyssop, Angelica, agrimony, sage, frankincense, and myrrh. He noticed his dog tags were wrapped around it and the chunk of hair Anna pulled out of his head was now the doll's hair.

Anna laid it in the middle of the table and poured four quadrants of white cornmeal creating a circle. She placed a white candle at the head, another at the feet.

"As I complete the ritual, Simon, focus all your thoughts on healing yourself and regaining your control."

She then placed a crucifix on the doll and splashed

it with holy water. She lit the candles and while they burned the women chanted a healing prayer. Once the candles burned down she indicated for Simon to follow her and they disposed of the wax in the running river water.

Anna and Simon returned happy and laughing.

"I have heard you'll be very tired and a nap will help to settle the magic," Berti said as she gathered items into her bag.

Yawning, he said, "Excuse me. Sorry about that. You're right, I am really tired."

"Take a nap, then come visit on the fourth day of the putsi and let me know how you feel," Anna said as she hugged him and collected her bags to leave.

Those ladies are fast he thought when minutes later, he was alone.

He stretched out on the couch and for the first time since returning, slept as a human.

Four Days Later

He had taken an all day run, wanting the exercise and needing to work off his raging hormones. After dinner and a quick shower he'd fallen to sleep on the couch.

Simon came awake to the most astonishing feeling of his life. He knew instinctively who was caressing him. Her scent was heavy in his nose and he loved it. Rose was stroking him...no woman had ever woken him in such a gentle manner. Her hand on his hair was warm, soothing. She stroked and smoothed it with tenderness, running her fingers through it over and over. And that meant more to him than anything. *She must not be mad at me anymore.*

He opened his eyes to the most beautiful sight. She was looking down at him with a smile on her full lips and a sparkle in her blue eyes. Her parted lips looked so inviting. So delicious…

Realizing he was awake she lifted his head from her lap and scooted off the couch. *Damn, I should have left ten minutes ago.* She hadn't wanted him to catch her petting his hair. He stood and she couldn't help but run her eyes over him. He was tall with lean defined muscles in his upper body, chest and arms, and wide shoulders. His hair was thick and dirty blond, some might call it shaggy sheik.

"That was nice, I could wake up to your pretty blue eyes every morning." He tucked in the edges of his shirt that escaped his jeans while he slept.

"I came by to see how you were feeling. Anna said you were sick and she had done something to make you feel better and it would help if I made sure you didn't have a fever. After I sat on the couch you rolled over and wriggled into my lap, I didn't want to wake you." She spoke rapidly and lowered her gaze.

He grinned to himself, *if I can make her this flustered I just might have a chance.* "Thank you for making sure I was okay, that means a lot to me. She told me to check in with her today, would you like company walking back?"

Her eyes shot back to his. "Um…Okay. Are you going right now?"

"Let me find my shoes and we'll be on our way."

He held her gaze and watched her grow a pretty pink under his scrutiny. He liked her flustered. He took her hands and searched her eyes. "I've missed you, Rose," he said in a hushed tone. "You're all I've been thinking about for days. I lie in bed and all I think about is seeing you, talking with you, touching you."

She pulled her hands free. He sensed irritation and unrest from her as she walked away from him. He gave her a moment to cool off while he put his shoes on.

"I don't get you, Simon," she said as she faced him. "You get upset if another man touches me and then you ditch me with two horny guys at your family barbeque. You avoid me for days and now you say you missed me and think about me all the time. What is wrong with you? Are you just playing with me? Because if you are…"

"Absolutely not. I've had issues that until now I couldn't control. I was sick, okay? Until the day you walked into Cade's house, I was nothing, simply existing. I got up, I ate, I worked, and I went to bed. Now… I want more, you make me want more."

"What kind of issues?" she asked quietly.

He ground his teeth in anger, wishing he could tell her the truth and have her believe it. But he couldn't. Not yet. "Someday I'll tell you all about it. But right now, I think we should see Cade and Anna."

He held the screen door open for her to precede him onto the deck, and then slid his palm down her arm to grasp her hand.

She stiffened for a second as she gazed at his face before looking away. Even though she obviously wanted him, she seemed uncomfortable with caresses and touching. *I'll have to delve into my mate's past, learn her secrets, and rid her of these physical uncertainties. At least she hasn't pulled her hand away,* he thought.

The two houses were on the same section of the plantation, just acres from each other. Too soon he released her hand to hold the door for her.

"Anna, we're here," Rose announced. Billiard balls cracking greeted them so they headed for the game room.

"Hi, guys," Anna said cheerfully as Cade growled at the solid that slipped into the side pocket. "Why, thank you, honey." She kissed his cheek as she passed him.

"I take it, you're stripes?" Simon asked.

"Yeah, Cade is getting his ass kicked by a girl," Stefan laughed.

"Oh, shut up." Cade snapped at him.

They all burst out laughing at his surly behavior over losing to his mate.

Anna polished off the eight ball and put her cue in the rack. "How are you feeling, Simon?"

"I feel amazing! I can't thank you enough."

"I'm still unclear about what illness you had," Rose chimed in.

Anna jumped in to cover for the men. "Sorry, Rose, that's kind of a private matter."

"Oh, yeah, I'm sorry. I didn't mean to pry." She looked mortified by her question.

"It's okay, cher. I'll explain it one day soon," Simon said, taking her hand, his wolf wanting to sooth her as much as the man did.

"Thank you, Simon." Rose stretched on tiptoes and placed a sweet kiss on his cheek. As she pulled back, she saw the way he savored it.

He picked her hand up and brought it to his lips, and placed a hungry kiss on her knuckles.

Rose glanced at the clock above the mantel. "I have some things I need to do in my room, so I'm going to call it a night. I'm glad you're feeling better, Simon. Goodnight everyone." She made a hasty exit to the safety of her bedroom.

Simon frowned as he watched her leave. "What the hell did I do now?" he asked Anna.

She shook her head and patted the couch cushion next to her. "You need to understand a few things about her."

The men gathered around Anna and waited for her to continue.

"She's had a rough life. Her parents died when she was so young, she doesn't remember them. During her years in foster care, well, let's just say she had some horrifying experiences. She doesn't trust men easily and hasn't had many relationships. I won't tell tales out of school, those are her stories to tell when she's ready. Just be patient with her and she'll come around as far as the physical aspects. She already desires you and has feelings for you. She hasn't had a lot of self-esteem until recently, you seem to have changed her in many ways. But you may need to tell her how you feel about her many times before she will believe it's true. Her heart and soul want you but her mind needs to catch up. She was making great strides until the barbeque; your disappearance sent her into a self-esteem tailspin. Are you prepared to hang in there for the long haul?" she asked Simon.

"I'm not going anywhere. I don't care how long it takes for her to believe she's the only one for me."

"Good answer. Now, Rose was right, it's getting late. Stop by in the morning for coffee and try again with her."

Chapter 8

The Picnic

Simon reluctantly trudged across the acreage between the houses. The further he got from Cade's the more his heart ached and his wolf howled. The weight on his chest was making it difficult to breathe. He felt pathetic when he only made it to the edge of the porch light's glow and had to turn back. Head hanging, he knocked on the door.

"Simon? Is everything all right?"

"I can't leave her." Short and to the point. No need to embarrass himself more than necessary.

"Come on, sweetheart. I have an empty guestroom." Graciously, Anna led him down the hall. The only other option would be sleeping outside Rose's door. Although explaining Simon rolled in a blanket on the floor in the hallway the next morning would have been interesting at best.

After failing to sleep all night, Simon stretched his tired and achy muscles. Being under the same roof with Rose only feet away, but in another room, had been torturous. He let out a happy chuckle. *I'll take the torture any day of the week.* In truth, being in a separate house from his mate wasn't an option so he wouldn't have it any other way.

Cocking his head, he heard her moving in her room. He scrambled to quickly grab his jogging pants from the end of the bed and tie the waist. He reached for his day old T-shirt but as he caught a whiff of it his head snapped back of its own accord and turned away. *Dear Goddess, that's disgusting*. He would just get a clean shirt after he had a cup of coffee. He tossed it back on the floor and stepped out of his room just as Rose was closing her door.

"Good morning, cher."

Startled, she let out a squeak in surprise.

"I'm sorry, I didn't mean to scare you."

She smiled then frowned as she recognized that deep, hypnotic voice. She looked over her shoulder to see Simon standing behind her. Wearing nothing but sweat pants, he was the best thing she'd ever seen. His blond hair was sleep mussed and a bit shaggy as it grew out from his military cut, and his blue eyes practically glowed. He took her breath away. *What the heck is he doing here?*

He had a manly voice. Rich and deep. It resonated with a Cajun drawl, and every time he spoke, it sent a strange chill through her. She'd never heard any man with a voice so innately masculine.

"Nice hair," she teased. "You're here very early…"

"It was getting late and Anna gave me a guest room for the night," he said, combing his hair with his fingers.

"Oh." Her eyes grew large. "That was nice of her."

"I thought so too." He shrugged, as they made straight for the aroma of coffee. He followed her into the kitchen. The entire house smelled of coffee and cinnamon rolls.

She poured herself a cup then looked at him. "Would you like some?"

"Yes, please."

Rose poured another cup and handed it to him. "Did I make it right? You take cream and sugar?"

"Perfect."

When he took it from her, she felt the warmth of his fingers brush hers.

An incredible rush went through her. She felt his surprise. His heated interest. *WHOA! What the heck was that?*

Tearing her gaze from his in shear self preservation, she noticed a note in the middle of the table.

Rose and Simon,

Both Cade and I were called to an important meeting. We will be gone most of the day.

Enjoy the rolls.

I heard the weather will be perfect today so I left a picnic lunch for you in the fridge. Choose any wine from the rack.

Have fun you two and see you at dinner.

Love,

Anna

Rose grinned while she grabbed a cinnamon roll from the plate. They smelled like a little slice of spicy heaven. She was munching happily on the roll and sipping her coffee when the delicate scent of fresh linens wafted around her. She glanced around the kitchen for a basket of freshly laundered sheets.

Where's that coming from? I love that smell.

They finished breakfast and sat in an uncomfortable silence sipping coffee.

I need to take this bull by the horns, he thought. "I'd love to have a picnic. Are you game?"

She hesitated. "I'm not sure that's such a good idea."

Simon frowned. "Why not?"

"I won't be here for long and…"

"Please, Rose, have lunch with me. I promise I will be a complete gentleman."

She studied him with a skeptical expression. "Okay, it could be fun. Anna's right, it does look like it'll be a nice day."

Simon gave her what could only be called a shit-eating grin. "I have a few things to do and then I'll come back for our lunch."

Offering him a smile, she said, "Perfect, I need to do laundry anyway."

A few hours later he returned. "Rose? Are you ready?" He called from the kitchen.

She popped her head out of the laundry. "In a minute, I'm folding the last load."

"I'll pack up the food, do you prefer red or white?" he asked.

"White would be wonderful, just give me a minute and I'll be ready."

A few minutes later he was holding the door for her as they left the house. He held the picnic basket in one hand and entwined his fingers with hers with the other. He could hear her heart racing and watched her throat work as she swallowed and avoided looking at him. She was such a fascinating contradiction of desire and hesitancy.

There was a gorgeous century old oak laden with Spanish moss close to his home that would be a wonderful location for their lunch date. The moss swayed in the breeze and dripped from the branches until it kissed the ground.

"Is this spot okay with you?" he asked.

He heard her suck in a breath and watched as a smile grew. "It's so pretty. I like the look of the moss in the trees down here. We don't have anything like it in Denver."

Taking the blanket from her, he spread it then helped her sit. Once she was comfortable he placed the basket by the edge and joined her. He tucked his arm behind his head as he lay back and searched the clouds. Simon reached for her hand again, this time slowly, gently, letting her get used to the idea. His fingers slid over hers in a caress. "I see a bear." *Goddess, her skin is incredible.*

She gave him a confused frown. "What?"

"In the clouds." He shielded his eyes and pointed. "See, right there? It's a bear."

Smiling excitedly, she lay next to him and searched for a shape. "I've never done this before."

"No way!"

"Really. In the houses I grew up in, there wasn't much of a yard and the parks weren't safe, so I never have."

"Well, then I'm honored to be the first to look for

cloud shapes with you. This will be just one of many firsts, I hope." He looked deeply into her eyes and lifted her knuckles to his lips.

She blushed a pretty shade of pink and avoiding his eyes, searched the clouds. "There!" She pointed excitedly. "A pony."

"You catch on fast." He gave her hand a squeeze.

They played the game for twenty minutes before a line of dark clouds filled the sky and the wind picked up. "I think we might get wet." She said scrutinizing the angry sky.

Suddenly lightning cut across the rolling darkness and thunder boomed. He jumped to his feet and quickly helped her off the blanket then scooped everything into his arms. "Run for my house." He nodded toward its direction.

They rushed for cover, almost outrunning the rain. Almost. The sky opened and sheets of rain came down, ten seconds more and they would have made it.

Like the last time she had been there, she almost missed seeing his house, a single level home with brick exterior and a wrap around porch. Lush green vines planted at the foundation scaled the brick, providing an effective camouflage. Given a few more years and the house would blend into the forest beautifully. *I wonder if this is an after effect of his military career.*

Her eyes shone bright with laughter, as she watched him juggle the food and blanket to open the door. His gaze grew hot as he held the door for her while balancing the picnic basket. She wondered why his expression changed and he became so intense as she ducked past him out of the downpour.

Dripping wet, she followed him to the kitchen. A small puddle formed where she stood. She could see into the living room and down a long wide hall to the other end of the home. The place was open and airy and *huge*.

Unpacking the basket with more earnest than was necessary, he pointed down the hall. "The bathroom is on the right side if you want it. Don't hurry on my account, though." He glanced quickly at her chest as a smile played at the edges of his lips.

She frowned. "Thank you, I'll be right back." She was soaked and really wanted to check her hair after their more than damp mad dash.

The bathroom was a sight to behold. Flagstone floors and teak cabinets, white-marble countertops and tub, a shower stall big enough for a small dinner party and soft, plush, white bath rugs. She scrunched her toes in the softness and wondered how they made a rug feel so incredible.

Heaven!

A linen closet provided matching white bath towels. She stared at herself in the vanity mirror, mortified that the rain had turned her blouse transparent. Now his behavior made a little more sense. There was a fluffy navy blue robe on a hook by the door. Biting her lip, she eyed it. *I hope he doesn't mind me borrowing this.* She slipped her arms into the sleeves, closed her eyes and sighed her pleasure. It was the finest thing she'd ever felt on her skin, lifting the lapels to her face she inhaled his fresh linen scent. Lightweight and so soft she couldn't think of a comparison. She dried her hair the best she could using her fingers as a comb.

When she opened the door, she found a basket filled with his sodden clothes on the floor along with a note to place hers in it too. Neatly folded next to the basket was a t-shirt and sweatpants. *Wow, what a thoughtful man.* She grudgingly put the robe back on the hook and changed into the clothes.

"Oh, good. You found them." He had a gleam in his eyes. "Would you like a tour?"

Embarrassed beyond mortification she didn't meet his gaze. "Um, sure." She was dying to see how he lived.

"I was overseas and only came home a few months ago." He sounded as if he were apologizing.

She noted as she walked through a series of large open rooms, he preferred floor to ceiling windows with the drapes opened wide to allow natural light to flood each room. The interior of Simon's house reflected his serviceman's past as much as the exterior had. *Minimalist R Us could hold meetings here.* She saw few frills, everything to meet his needs without clutter, sparse but refreshingly clean. *Huh, I like this, I guess what you see is what you get with him. Perfect, I hate games.*

"I love your house. I've never had much for possessions and learned to live on the essentials, so your clutter-free style makes me feel right at home."

"I would like to hear about your life, Rose, if you're willing to tell me about it."

I barely know him. What will he think? I have a strange feeling I should tell him something. Well, I don't have to tell him everything...

She sank into one of the recliners, avoiding his eyes. Breathing a heavy sigh, she said, "Are you going to sit?" She looked up with a spark of challenge in her gaze.

Simon's silver-blue eyes wavered between the couch and his other recliner, and something inside her softened and warmed. "If it would make you feel better." He settled for the recliner facing her and waited.

"I've never fit in anywhere," she began. "I was orphaned before I could walk. Even though I was still a baby and very adoptable, none of the families wanted me. I never understood why. Still don't, but gave up trying to figure that out long ago. After a while, I accepted my situation and focused on getting to my eighteenth birthday and on my own. Anna and her sons, along with my foster brothers Jack and Michael, are the only people who have ever honestly cared about me. Even the men I've dated didn't truly care about Rose the person, they were just after…you know. They would say all the pretty words and dole out the compliments but it was all for show." She picked at invisible lint on the chair. "I've been alone for a long time."

A frown creased his brow, the disapproval evident in his gorgeous eyes. "How long have you been alone, Rose?"

"I'm thirty eight." She felt better stating her age rather than the number of years spent feeling like an outcast.

"You never need to be alone again," he whispered. "And those men were morons."

He was staring at her. *Has he even blinked?* It was rather unnerving. "Why are you staring?"

"Because you're beautiful." He must have seen her stiffen in reaction to his compliment. "Sorry. I didn't mean to make you feel uncomfortable." He sat up and looked pointedly at her before a smile lifted his sensual lips. He held out his hand. "Come on, I set the food on the table, would you like to join me for some long overdue lunch?"

She laughed and found herself relaxing a bit. "I'd love to, I'm starving." Taking a seat, she filled her plate. "So, Simon, what about you? What's your story?"

She was incredibly curious about the man sitting across from her. She was sure he was attracted to her, though she had precious little experience with men. At least not the pleasant or welcomed kind. The feeling was mutual, but she was on untested ground. She wanted to pursue him desperately but didn't know how. *What did he like in women? A demur, quiet lady? A sizzling sex kitten? Pfff, yeah, like I could pull that off. NOT.*

Filling his own plate he began, "I'm afraid mine's pretty boring. I'm the sixth of seven sons. Most of us have built homes here on the plantation," he explained. "There's Cade, Stefan, and Marcus, who you've met. Lucas, Seth, and Brian are traveling but should be coming home soon."

"Anna said you were in the service?"

"Yes, I recently returned from four years in the Middle East with the Marines."

"Was that difficult? Did you see any action?"

"It was very difficult and someday I'll tell you all about it. Right now, I'd rather enjoy your company."

Okay, no asking about his military past. Check. She wanted to know more but she wouldn't press. They fell into a conversation of basic friendly chitchat. The kinds of things people talk about on first dates.

She noticed he listened closely to what she had to say. He watched her with an intensity that was beginning to unnerve her. Men, who looked at her like that, eventually tried things she didn't welcome. *Simon isn't like those men.* She smiled secretly to herself as her heart fluttered excitedly.

Placing her napkin on the table, she stood. As he rose to help, she quickly said, "You stay sitting, I'll clean up. It's a universal rule, the host doesn't wash the dishes."

She stacked the plates, and then halted, eyeing the narrow gap between Simon and the cabinets, why did this room need to be so skinny? She would have to pass him to reach the sink, *Boobs or butt? Butt.*

She turned her back to him and slid her behind across his already engorged manhood as she squeezed by. Mid-squeeze, his lips were right next to her ear when he sucked in his breath and let out a groan. Instant wet panties. She now understood the description of having butterflies in your stomach. *Well if that isn't the most delightful and yet uncomfortable feeling.* She was breathing heavily from a five-foot walk across the room, *you'd think I had just run a marathon.* She gripped the cold porcelain sink like a survivor from the Titanic gripped a lifejacket. *That man is way too potent.*

Except for the epic groan, Simon hadn't spoken during her offer to wash the dishes. Staring down at the running water, she felt the air move behind her. *How did he get behind me without making a sound?*

She stole a glance at him in the reflection of the window. Her eyes clashed with his intense unblinking stare. They glowed in the dimly lit room. Tensing she thought, *eyes don't glow like that.* Then she reached for an excuse. *Maybe the light is hitting them at an odd angle.*

She watched, mesmerized as Simon's eyes glowed even hotter the moment his fingertips touched the bare skin of her shoulder. They felt calloused, what had caused them to be so rough? *Hardened by work maybe.* The roughened skin raised a trail of goose bumps as they skimmed down her arm and up again. She throbbed between her legs. No man had ever turned her on like this. Of course, she had allowed only a handful of men to get near enough to her to touch her sexually.

Simon's arm brushed hers as he reached past to turn the water off. A burst of electric sparks danced across her skin. She closed her eyes and breathed deeply as his scent enveloped her in a cloud of fresh linen.

With his breath warm on her neck and his teeth lightly scraping the skin she heard *MINE* growled in her mind.

Her eyes flew open in shock to lock onto his reflected still glowing gaze.

And his very long, very sharp teeth.

Too late, he snapped his mouth shut and turned from her view.

Spinning away, she stumbled from the sink and Simon. "What was that?" she squeaked.

She saw a dimmer switch and in a mad impulse turned the lights all the way up.

Looking away, he said, "Rose, please let me explain." When he looked at her again his eyes were no longer glowing. When his lips parted his teeth were back to normal.

"I thought Anna would have told you." There was a long pause.

"Told me what?"

"That I'm a shifter."

"A what?"

"I can shift shape from human to wolf."

"Shut the front door!"

"Shut the…? What?" Now he looked confused.

"Never mind, it's a saying." She waved at the door then crossed her arms. "Shifters aren't real. Everyone knows that. So, out with it, what just happened here? Your eyes were glowing funky and I swear I heard you in my head. Are you sure you're not a vampire? You certainly have wicked fangs like one." She was babbling.

"Vampire? You believe in vampires but not shifters?" he asked.

"Of course, I've met a vampire. I know they're real."

"When did you meet a vampire?" he growled.

"When Anna and I went into town, one named Etienne saved me from some muggers."

He grabbed her by the shoulders. "What the hell, Rose! You were mugged!"

"Geez, Simon, calm down. I told Cade all about it when we got back. They're taking care of it."

"You should have told me."

"Why?"

"Because, it's my responsibility to protect you."

"Since when am I your responsibility? I. Am. No. Man's. Responsibility." She emphasized each word with a poke to his ribs.

"You are. You're my mate. That means I'm responsible for your safety."

She stepped back from him. "I'm your what? You make me sound like a dog or something."

"This has gone all wrong." He scrubbed his hands through his hair. "There's no going back now so I'll just prove to you I can shift and then explain everything to you, okay?"

"Yeah, sure. Let's see you turn into a wolf," she scoffed.

"I'm telling you the truth. Watch." A huge wolf stood before her.

And ear splitting scream preceded her dash for the door. As she crossed the lawn, skirting the woods, she heard Simon curse in her mind.

Shit, I'm such a dumb ass, I should've thought that through.

Chapter 9

Explaining to Rose

Rose was looking over her shoulder when she heard a growl emanate from the tree line. Her eyes snapped to the forest as a mangy brown wolf stepped from the shadows, followed by a grey wolf. Her lungs erupted in a blood-curdling scream as she skidded to a halt. Snarling wolves in front of her and footsteps pounding behind her. Trapped!

The grey wolf growled and bared its teeth as it leapt between her and the brown wolf. She stumbled back, away from their snapping jaws. A stone beneath her shoe sent her to the ground. She was scuttling backwards on her backside as fast as she could when Simon appeared in front of her.

He crouched between her and the growling wolves, his lips pealed back in a vicious snarl.

She gasped at the horrible sound coming from him and froze. For the first time in her life, she was so terrified she couldn't move.

The wolf nearest her immediately crouched in submission and the mangy wolf ran, disappearing into the forest.

Simon used his body as a shield and remained solidly between her and the cowering grey wolf. "Shift. Now!" he demanded.

Startled, she screamed and clutched Simon's leg. Her eyes grew wide as she registered the fact that a wolf had just become an older man.

Averting his gaze, "Forgive me, my lord, I meant no harm."

Simon remained in his attack stance. "Tell me who you are and what you are doing on Le Beau land."

"I'm Jason Ledet." He bowed and kept his gaze low. "I followed my nephew Travis onto your land. My prince, your brother, Lord Cade tasked me to be responsible for Travis's actions. I beg you to pardon this unforgivable intrusion."

With the threat alleviated, he relaxed slightly. "Why would he come here?" Simon scowled.

Jason snuck a glance at Rose before fixing on the ground again. "Travis can become confused, erratic. His mind is no longer … right." He hesitated. "He must be constantly watched."

"Mr. Ledet, look at me," he demanded. "Why is his mind 'not right,' as you say?" Simon's gaze pinned the older man to the spot.

It was like watching an ant squirm under a magnifying glass. "He has a singularly unique gift." He visibly struggled to not look away then cleared his throat. "He's the first shifter of record to be born a blocker. He has a very bad habit of using his gift against other shifters, then being sentenced to blood rights. The repeated blows to his head have adversely affected him."

Simon frowned. "What's a blocker?"

"He can block any shifter from using their gift against him. Worse yet, he can prevent them from using their gift at all." Curling his lip back from his fangs. "He has prevented one mate from speaking to the other telepathically."

Simon gasped, his eyes wide.

What are they talking about? she wondered.

On shear instinct, Simon's arm snaked out and snatched her from the ground to his side.

She squeaked and stood stiffly against him. He smelled her fear and his wolf snarled, angry at his treatment of its mate.

"That's not possible," he all but whispered.

"I'm sorry to say, it is. His supervision has been a hardship to say the least. When his parents passed, it fell to me to oversee his 'behavior,' and attempt to keep him in line."

"How dangerous is he? Do I need to put additional security in place?"

Jason dropped his gaze to his feet. "I'll make every attempt to keep him away from this part of the bayou." He shuffled his feet nervously.

"But…?"

"Once he gets something into his head, he sees it through no matter the consequences."

That had Simon growling. "What, exactly, has he gotten into his head?"

"I don't know yet. Even as addled as he is, he's still quite cunning."

"Thank you for protecting, Rose, I apologize for misunderstanding the situation. Do what you can with Travis and keep me informed."

"I'm honored to protect the mate of one of my princes." He bowed so low his nose almost grazed the grass. A moment later as a grey wolf, he bounded into the forest and out of sight.

Now alone, Simon turned his gaze to his mate. He cringed when he saw the terror written on her face. He lifted his hand to brush the hair from her eyes but she cowered from his touch. "I'm so sorry, Rose…"

Before he could finish speaking she tore from his arms and ran to the safety of Anna's house.

SHIT!

Simon jerked his cell phone from his pocket. "Cade, how quickly can you and Anna be home?"

"We have about another hour of work, why?"

"I need you and Anna to talk to Rose about shifters. There was an incident and she saw me shift. I scared her, Cade. My mate is terrified of me. Then it got worse when two other shifters came at her from the forest."

"Dieu sacrebleu!" Cade covered the phone. "Anna, we're leaving immediately." Then he spoke to Simon again. "Twenty minutes, hang tight."

He stopped his pacing for the hundredth time to see if Cade's car had returned.

Simon rubbed his chin in thought. *How am I going to explain everything to Rose without scaring her back to Denver? Where do I even begin? After what she's seen and heard she may never speak to me again.*

The sound of a car in the driveway had him bursting onto his front porch. Cade signaled him to stay put while he and Anna went into the house.

Rose rushed to the front door the moment she heard the car pull up. Anna was still a good two feet from the door when Rose threw it open and dragged her inside.

"Hurry, there's a werewolf out there! We need to get Cade inside!"

Anna hugged her tight and shushed her like a baby. "It's okay, hun. There isn't a werewolf outside. You saw Simon shift."

It took a few seconds for that to sink in. "What? You knew he was a monster and left me with him!"

Cade stepped through the door as Rose broke from Anna's arms and glared, confused and angry at her best friend.

"Calm down and just breathe for a minute. I'll explain everything just like I did with Etienne." Anna said as she reached for Rose's arm and led her to the couch.

Cade was about to speak when Anna put one finger to her lips. *Let me know when you want me to help explain.* Anna had this under control.

"Would you like something to drink while I tell you about us?" Anna asked calmly.

"Yes, a VERY strong whiskey coke. NO, make it a double, better yet a triple. Wait, what? Anna? Us?!"

Cade can you get her that drink asap?

Sure, cher

"Yes, sweetheart, US. All of the Le Beaus are shifters, including me. When Cade and I completed the mating ritual I was converted. Long ago, shifters were created by a Goddess. They only have half of their soul and their destined mate has the other half. I am Cades mate and you are a shifter mate as well."

Anna paused as Cade handed Rose a VERY strong drink and his mate a glass of sweet tea.

"We aren't werewolves like in the movies. Shifters change or shift at will and we don't attack people. We are basically humans who live a long time, have a few magical qualities or should I say abilities, and can change into a wolf."

Rose took a gulp of her drink and eyeballed Cade. "You are absolutely sure they don't bite when they go all furry? Or have I gone insane and your just keeping me calm until the men in white coats show up?"

"Cade would you please shift for her and let her pet you?"

You are going to owe me for this. He growled suggestively into her mind.

"Are you ready, Rose? I would hate to scare you."

Rose scooted closer to Anna. "Okay, I'm ready."

Suddenly Cade the wolf stood before her wagging his tail.

"You can pet him, hun, he is still human inside. He can think and control his actions just like he does in human form."

Rose hesitated glancing between Anna and the wolf when Cade stepped to her and rested his head next to her on the couch still wagging his tail.

She gingerly touched him with only her fingertips at first. "He's so soft," she said quietly.

As she became more comfortable with the wolf at her feet, she petted him in long sweeping glides.

"Simon will be frantic by now. He's very worried about you and concerned that you won't speak to him again."

"I'm okay now…I think. He shocked the heck out of me and when the other wolves showed up snarling and all drooly I freaked. But I'm good now."

He stared at their house and prayed for a sign from Cade. He didn't hear any screaming or crying, that had to be good, right? He raked his hands through his hair again, in frustration. If he kept this up he would be bald by dinner.

An excruciating forty-five minutes later Cade walked across the yard. "Are you holding it together?"

"Barely. Is she okay?"

"Anna calmed her down and we explained shifters to her. She believes you're a shifter now. You'll still have to explain what a mate is and that she's yours, our rules and magic as well as the ritual." He glared at Simon. "She made me shift because she thought she had gone insane and made it all up."

With hands on hips he hung his head. "What should I do, Cade?"

"She's ready to see you again. Take it slow, her nerves are stretched very thin. And before you try to complete the ritual, you and I are having a talk."

"Why? Is there something I need to worry about?"

"The effects of the ritual on women over thirty is different than younger women. I'll explain it later, for now, go see your mate." He clapped Simon on the back and walked with him to the house.

As they entered the great room, Cade reached for his mate. "Come on, cher, Simon and Rose need privacy."

Simon entered the room slowly, afraid fast movements would set her off. The scent of stress and anxiety rolled from her in waves.

"Rose, please don't be afraid of me," he begged.

"I'm not afraid of you, at least not anymore. You scared the crap out of me, though. I dread the dreams I'll have tonight."

"I'll hold you and keep the nightmares away, if you let me," he whispered.

"In your dreams," she quipped.

"May I sit with you?"

She patted the cushion next to her on the couch.

He hesitantly joined her. As he reached for her hand he stopped and searched her eyes. "May I hold your hand?"

She chuckled. "You don't need to worry that I'll run screaming from the room. I have it together now."

He breathed a sigh of relief and took her hand.

"Obviously, I believe you now. You can indeed turn into a wolf. And, it seems there is a lot I don't know about you," she said as she sank further into the couch.

He nodded and looked ashamed as he met her gaze, then a frown creased his brow. "I really am sorry. I thought Anna would have told you about us by now. I know she wasn't supposed to, but you are the closest she has to a sister. I thought you were just staying quiet about it."

She put her hand up like a stop sign. "I'm not sure I'm ready to hear all of the wolf details, but I do have a few questions."

He liked the idea of her leading the conversation with questions. Maybe he would avoid being an idiot again. "Okay, what can I explain for you?"

"Don't get me wrong, I'm not forgetting about you sprouting fur, but start with the whole prince thing, and we'll go from there." She had one brow cocked like she'd caught him in a lie.

"Technically, my family is the royalty of the shifters. I've never seen the actual pomp and circumstance it used to involve. My parents ceased that before I was born. I wasn't aware we were still considered the royal family until today."

"So, Isaac is the king. Is Cade automatically the next king?"

"I guess so, like I said it all ended before I was born and we never really talk about it."

"Do I need to be worried about that crazy guy Travis?"

"I'll be calling a meeting with the family. I'd like you there as well. We do need to prepare for his return, to follow through on whatever it is he's set his mind to. I'm not sure who or what that is yet, so I can't truthfully answer you. I will say, I don't want you outside the house alone until this is dealt with." The more agitated he became the more he rubbed his thumb across the back of her hand.

"Oh, you don't need to worry about that. He scared me to death. But you might want to ease up on my knuckles before they start to bleed."

"Oh my god, I'm so sorry. I had no idea I was doing that. Did I hurt you?"

"No, I'm fine." Rose shook her head, her long blond hair tumbling over her shoulders. She chuckled and patted his hand to emphasize her point.

"Can you explain what a mate is? Cade and Anna told me she's one and I am too. Whose mate am I?"

Sheepishly he looked her in the eye. "You're my mate. I told you in my kitchen, but you were pretty upset and must not remember. I knew the moment we met, I just wasn't sure how to explain all the wolf stuff and being a mate is a part of that. A shifter only has one mate in the world, needless to say it's rare to find each other against those odds. A mate is like a spouse for a human but so much more. Do you want me to explain it now or when you're ready to hear all the 'wolf stuff'?"

Rose had turned a vibrant shade of pink. "Does that make me your girlfriend?"

"My girlfriend and a whole lot more." His voice was gentle and soothing. A slow smile tugged at his lips. "Now that I'm your boyfriend do I get to kiss you?"

The look of longing on his face tore through her. "I guess so," she shyly whispered. She felt a strange wrenching in her chest as her soul reached for his, crying out for its mate, recognizing its other half. She didn't understand what she was feeling or what it meant.

He cupped her cheek with his palm. The softness of her skin amazed him. It also made him hard enough to pound nails.

She leaned into his touch and offered her lips to his. Her trust hit him like a sledgehammer and left him oddly dazed. She cocked her head as if studying him in turn.

With his heart hammering in his chest he gently brushed his lips to hers.

He felt her hands creep up his chest tentatively and it added fuel to his desire. His palm slid into her hair as he deepened the kiss.

He reluctantly pulled back, groaning when her teeth tugged at his lower lip. Good Lord, this must be punishment for some past sin. He was so aroused his jeans nearly cut off his circulation.

Her eyes opened and her entire body trembled. Her gaze held such a deep-seeded desire, it rocked him.

Savoring having his mate's trust once again, he held her in his arms for a minute longer. She was a gorgeous woman with a beautiful heart and soul who was also barely more than a stranger. Since the moment she'd been introduced to him at the Thanksgiving feast and they'd locked eyes with each other, he'd been on a rapid road to recovery. The knowledge they were mates had been the shock his system needed to put it into high gear. He had swiftly returned to himself and his loved ones, and now he was back completely.

He knew Rose had lived a lonely life. He was determined to give her everything she'd missed out on. A home, safety, and people she could call family and count on.

He leaned back and swept a tendril of hair from her cheek. "I'm so thankful for you, Rose." He kissed her gently once again. "It's still early, would you like to have dinner with me? I'd like to take you on a proper date."

"I'd love to."

Looking down into her enormous blue eyes, Simon felt like he was falling forward into a deep, beautiful pool.

Her gaze locked with his. Her body reacted, shuddering.

The way he kept eye contact, he wasn't letting her look away. Taking her hand, he raised her palm and laid it over his heart.

Rose swallowed hard and blinked up at him, all too aware of his muscles beneath his shirt. Aware of his heart beat. Aware of the heat from his skin. She felt mesmerized by him.

"I'll be back with my car in two hours. Jeans and T-shirt are fine." He gave her one last lingering kiss and left.

Like clockwork, Simon knocked on the door for his first of many dates with his mate. "Ready?"

"Yes, and starving too."

"Close your eyes, I have a surprise." He took her by the hand and led her to the driveway. "Okay, you can open them." He heard her gasp when she saw his vintage Chevelle SS convertible. Candy apple red with black interior and the top was down.

"I love this car!" she squealed as she ran to get a closer look. She caressed the hood with just her fingertips. The way she was touching and looking at it, he wanted to be his car right then.

He opened the passenger door sweeping his arm dramatically. "Climb in and I'll take you for a spin. There's a diner not far from here but we can take a quick drive before dinner."

Once he cleared the driveway and had a stretch of asphalt in front of him, he let her rip. He laughed as she threw her arms out like in the movie Thelma and Louise.

Simon was torn between watching the road and watching his mate, as she enjoyed every second of the ride. She was a plus sized beauty, perfectly proportioned. He was having a hard time focusing on his driving and not on the fascinating fact that the wind plastered her shirt to her body. He could see the exact shape of her beautiful breasts, the outline of her puckered nipples as they strained against the thin, tight material. He licked his lips, unable to stop looking at them. She had tucked the cotton shirt into the waistband of her jeans, and it called his attention to the curve of her hip.

She had her head thrown back, her thick, blond hair streamed in the wind. He could see her neck and the outline of her body beneath the shirt, almost as if she wore nothing at all. His body stirred, hardened. Simon didn't bother to fight his reaction. He admired the flawless perfection of her skin. Imagined the way she would feel beneath his fingertips, his palms.

Rose's head suddenly snapped up and she crossed her arms. Her breasts ached, felt swollen and hot, and deep inside, a sexual appetite began to stir. Simon was watching the road, his hands on the steering wheel, but she *felt* his hands on her body. Sweeping caresses, his palms cupping her breasts, thumbs stroking her nipples until she was shivering in awareness and hunger.

She couldn't help seeing the rigid length bulging beneath his jeans, and he made no effort to hide it. His unashamed display sent her body into overtime with its reaction. She bit her lip and imagined what he looked like naked, what he'd feel like under her tongue.

She tore her gaze away when she felt the car slowing to enter the diner's parking lot.

"I've requested their private room, we can enjoy dinner and I can answer the questions I feel rolling around in your mind." He said in a husky voice as he opened her door and presented his hand. The owner gave Simon a nod and escorted them to their private table.

They enjoyed a wonderful hearty gumbo and were now sipping wine. He rolled the wine on his tongue as he devoured her with his eyes. He wanted to get her home where he could kiss her again.

"Simon, Anna mentioned abilities shifters have. What did she mean?"

"There are several generally known powers. Shifting into a wolf, which you have already seen. We also have the ability to dress or undress with a thought, instantaneously. We heal ten times faster than humans and we can move so rapidly, the human eye can't detect us. As mates we can talk telepathically and send caresses or feelings of emotion through the use of magic. Plus, each shifter is born with one additional gift. The ability manifests during childhood."

"Holy mackerel! My head is spinning from all that."

"Let's take them one at a time, how about we try the telepathy. I'll send you a message, so when you hear me don't freak out."

She looked leery. "Okay...."

You look amazing tonight.

Her eyes got huge. "I think I really heard you."

"Send something back to me, just think it at me."

You're the most amazing man I've ever met.

Well, thank you, Rose. I think you are pretty amazing too.

"Wow, this could be useful. So, no one else can hear me but you?"

"No, you can only hear your mate. Let me try one more thing." He caressed her hand with his thoughts.

She gasped and pulled her hand back. "Was that you?"

He gave her a wry grin. "It sure was, you try it. Imagine touching me."

She closed her eyes and concentrated. When she opened them he was smiling and had his hand on his cheek. "I felt that."

He was thrilled to see the shine of excitement in her eyes. "Let's leave the rest for another time. I don't want to overwhelm you after the day you've had."

They finished their wine and hopped into his car for another ride. Rose was like a child in her exuberance. She was leaning back with her arm out the side of the car catching the wind.

His eyes instantly feasted on her taut nipples from the cooling night air. This was his new favorite car. Naturally, he began to imagine the way her breasts would feel in his palm.

Rose's eyes shot to him, a look of shock on her face. "Stop touching my breasts." Faint color stole under her skin.

He held up his hands in surrender. "I have no idea what you're talking about."

"You know *exactly* what I'm talking about."

She felt his palm cupping her breast, a thumb stroking her nipple until she shivered with hunger. "You mean, that?"

"Yes, that. I still feel you touching me."

He nodded and frowned a little. "I consider myself an innocent victim to your charms. I've always had control, in fact I took pride in my self-discipline. You have destroyed it. Permanently."

She felt his hunger as he devoured her with his eyes. With his mind. He ran his tongue over his teeth, and she felt it across her nipple.

Rose's breath hissed out. She was thrilled by his touch and yet a little terrified by her body's reactions.

"One day soon I'll convince you to show them to me," he growled.

His bold behavior fueled her own. She turned toward him, panting. "Keep that up and I may do just that. You have seen breast before, right? Mine are no different than any other woman's." There was color in her face and her breath came fast. "You know, I once heard that men thought about sex every sixty seconds but you must be setting some kind of record."

"They aren't just any breasts, Rose. They're YOUR breasts. And if you keep teasing me, I'm going to dare you to take that blasted T-shirt off." She heard him take a shuddering breath and as he reached for the blinker, his hand shook. She must have really rattled him.

She bit her lip and looked at him from the corner of her eye. *Should I? They're just boobs.* She took a quick glance to make sure no one else would see her. *Not a soul in sight. I could flash him? Hell, like Jack*

124

*always tells me if you do something do it all the way.
Grinning secretly to herself she took a deep breath...*

Simon nearly ran off the road as she pulled her shirt off.

He swallowed hard. "I don't think that was a good idea."

Rose realized instantly she might have been a bit impulsive. His blue eyes began to glow, raging with a hungry fever. His hand gripped the wheel until small cracks appeared. Sexual heat leapt between them, fierce and passionate. She wanted to rip his shirt away, and feel his hands, his mouth, sliding over her skin. She wanted things she'd never dreamed or thought of. Had no idea she craved.

Her breasts were even fuller than he'd thought, jutting forward to tempt him. She was beautiful. Her skin was amazing.

Thankfully, his house was hidden from the others. He didn't need to show off his half naked mate to the family. The car skidded to a stop, practically at the foot of his deck stairs. He leapt from it without bothering with the door. Simon raced to her side and lifted her out too. Like a streak of lightning, he sped to the door and opened it with such urgency, it almost came off its hinges.

With Rose in his arms, he marched straight to his bedroom and kicked the door closed.

The wall he had built between them melted. He set her on his bed. Breathing hard, he forced himself to be the man he was raised to be. "Mon amour, if you aren't ready for this, if you want me to stop, you need to tell me now."

She shook her head. "I've wanted you since the first moment I saw you."

She nibbled on her lower lip.

"What is it, cher?"

"I haven't been with anyone for a long time and it's never been the best experience for me," she said it quickly as if to get it over with.

"Oh, baby. That just makes this all the more special. I'll be gentle and make it incredible. I promise."

She nodded still sucking on her lip.

He made sure he had her full attention, and then he thought his clothes away. He wanted to let her look her fill and waited for her anxiety to dissipate before he joined her on the bed.

Oh, dear lord! She couldn't breathe as she got her first look at him. She'd known he would have a great body, but this... It exceeded everything from her dreams. His broad shoulders tapered to a washboard stomach that could be used for laundry. He had a six-pack that rippled with every breath he took. His entire torso was lightly covered by hair, making him look even more masculine. She saw a drop of moisture bearing witness to his urgent need. It was all she could do not to drool.

He wrapped her in his arms as he laid himself next to her, his bare chest rubbing against her breasts through her lace bra. It created a delicious friction against her nipples. His hands tunneled in the wealth of her silken hair, fisted, as if he had to make sure she didn't escape. He leaned in, his gaze as fierce and intent as the tension surrounding them. He eased her lips toward his. His mouth fastened onto hers, took possession. She felt heat leap from her to him, need raged between them. The kiss went on and on. He pulled back slightly and seemed to search her gaze.

"I have wanted you since the moment I saw you."

She reached up and laced her fingers in his hair. The heat of his blue eyes scorched her. He dipped his head until his lips hovered dangerously close to hers, as if he were asking her permission to continue.

Breathless, she responded with her actions. She closed the distance and laid her lips against his. He growled deep in his throat before his kiss turned hungry, passionate.

His tongue slid into her mouth, danced a long, sensual tango. His mouth moved over hers, demanding. Urgent and wild. The back of her head fit nicely in his palm and he held her to him, kissing her soft lips, her chin, her neck where he would bite her during the ritual. He nuzzled her then returned to her mouth again. His body hardened until he thought he would split. He *had* to have her. Had to make her his.

Her scent drew him. It was impossible to think or reason with her tongue teasing his, her teeth nibbling at his lips and his shoulder. He kissed his way down her throat and across her collarbone. Felt her gasp as he lapped at her nipple through the lace. Heard her breath explode from her lungs as he fastened his mouth over her breast. She moaned inarticulately, and her hands came up to cradle his head. She arched so he could reach under her to unclasp her bra and draw it off.

"You are so beautiful," he said, his voice deep and hungry. They were a lush bounty. Puckered and swollen, they overflowed his hands. He'd never seen anything more beautiful. She laced her hands in his hair while he dipped his head to suckle her. Closing his eyes, he groaned in pleasure as he ran his tongue around her puckered nipple. He feasted on her tender exposed flesh, devoured her. Still he needed more. He needed her completely naked, desperate to get to her, desperate to have all of her. With a thought she was gloriously naked to his starved gaze.

"Simon!" she inhaled and then turned red from her scalp to her toes.

"Magnificent."

His wolf's soul wanted to taste her. It wanted to breathe her in and let her softness ease the loneliness that had filled his heart these past years. He hadn't touched a woman sexually in over four years—a record for him. Midnight fantasies of him taking her in every position known had tortured him since Thanksgiving. Dreams of him exploring every single inch of her succulent body.

He slipped his mouth from her breast to lap at her skin, teasing every nerve ending, as he tasted his way to her triangle of curls. He wanted her head spinning, dizzy with need, with hunger. Her moan was music to his ears.

Simon rested his forehead on her stomach for just a moment, trying to catch his breath. His hands trembled as he caressed her skin. He wanted to go slow, to make this first time perfect for Rose, but his wolf wanted to ravage her, drag her into his arms and devour her. He forced himself to slow down, using his years of discipline to savor the softness of her skin. To hear her small gasps as he kissed his way along the curve of her hip and the nip of her waist. His tongue teased each rib and found the underside of her breast.

"Mmmmm, more." She arched into him. Rose ran her hands over his chest, her fingertips traced over and around his hardened nipples.

Simon moaned. "You have magic fingers, my love."

He skimmed his tanned hand down her belly, whispered over her thighs, and touched her intimately. Rose groaned at the sensation of his long, tapered fingers separating the tender folds of her body so he could caress her. She moved restlessly, needing more. Aching in places she didn't know she had. He gently sank his fingers deep inside her.

Rose nearly arched off the bed. "Simon, it's too much." But her body said something else, she had two handfuls of his hair, her hips were moving restlessly in invitation."

He was kissing his way up her ribcage, and nibbled his way around her plump breast. "The beauty of making love correctly is that you aren't supposed to stay in control. I want you to let go, scream my name and explode in ecstasy around me." His breath was hot against her nipple, teasing it into a tight peak. "Relax and enjoy every sensation and allow yourself to feel, to completely submit to the pleasure." He said as he closed his mouth around a taut peak.

She cried out, wrapping her arms around his head to cradle him to her. There was only Simon with his sinful mouth and his masterful hands and the sheer pleasure coursing through her body.

He looked up with a hot, consuming, intense stare. His hands were everywhere, caressing, plucking, plumping, and pleasing her. His mouth moved over her breast, nuzzled her nipple and flicked it with his tongue. Each time he pulled at her breast a fresh trickle of warm welcoming liquid glistened invitingly between her legs.

One hand glided up her thigh, cupped her. His finger slipped in.

"You're so tight, cher, and so hot. I want you dripping and ready for me, feeling only pleasure and no discomfort."

"Please, Simon you're driving me crazy."

"As you wish." He grinned wickedly and sensuously slid down her body planting kisses then with a hungry gleam in his eyes, lowered his head between her thighs. His hands held her hips in place and he began his assault.

If she had any thoughts before, they were scattered in all directions now. A gasp escaped as she tried to arch off the bed but he held her in place. "I can't take anymore." She was going to shatter into a million pieces. She heard her own cry, a raw shout of pure passion she couldn't suppress as tremors shook her.

Simon rose and covered her, his wide shoulders blocked out everything in the room as he nudged her thighs wider to accommodate him. She pushed forward, desperate to feel him inside her. Every single part of her body throbbed for him.

"I'll be careful, Rose. I'll use a condom and make sure there's little chance you'll get pregnant." He reached for the bedside table drawer.

"You don't have to worry about getting me pregnant." She wanted him deep inside her more than she wanted anything. He didn't move, pressing against her and driving her wild. "I'm on birth control."

His head reared back, his blue eyes moving over her face. Wary. Almost angry. "Why the hell would you be on birth control if you aren't sleeping with anyone? Who, Rose?"

She stared back at him for a long moment. "Are you insane? You're going to get jealous because I'm on birth control when I told you it's been a long time since I've been with a man?"

Simon groaned. His body was on fire with need, was as hard as it could be, and he was arguing with her over something utterly ridiculous. Of course she wasn't sleeping with anyone, and what difference would it make if she had before she met him? He hardly recognized his own primitive reactions. The mating instinct had to be stimulating every reaction and heightening his senses and emotions. "Yes, I'm insane," he admitted. "I want you so much I don't even know what the hell I'm saying anymore. I apologize for being a complete idiot."

"Then shut up and kiss me. And for God's sake, make love to me before I become a puddle of goo."

He leaned down as she strained upward to find his mouth with hers. He kissed her with every fiber of his being, a hot blend of passion and possession. Their mouths clung together until she fell back, her hips rising to meet the slow thrust of his. He was stretching her, pushing through her hot, slick folds, burying his body deep to join them together. He felt thick and hard and too big for her body. The burning increased as he thrust deeper.

"Oh God." She didn't know if it was a protest or a plea. Lights were dancing behind her eyelids. She lifted her hips, and drove herself onto him. The world as she'd always known it crumbled away as waves of intense pleasure rocked her body.

She clung to him, digging her fingers into his shoulders to anchor herself in some reality.

He gripped her hips and pulled her toward him as he surged into her over and over. He let himself go with it, burying himself deep in the haven of her body.

He felt her body tightening around his, the small muscles gripping and clamping as he increased the pace, adding to the friction and the wealth of heat and fire. He didn't want it to end. He never wanted it to end, but her body was already rippling with life, a strong orgasm that rushed over her like a tidal wave and carried him with her.

A harsh, hoarse cry tore from his throat. His fingers tightened as he released himself into her, thrusting hard, wanting to be as deep inside her as he could get. He lay over her, unable to move. Capturing her breast in his mouth, he felt the exquisite clamping of her muscles around him in another explosive shock wave.

Rose breathed heavily. "This was the most incredible sex I've ever had."

"Then I did it right." He panted as he took her hand and relaxed next to his sated mate.

Chapter 10

Rose's Past

Simon woke with his mate in his arms, he smiled and snuggled her closer. How could he be so blessed? *Thank you, Goddess.*

He dozed for another hour until he felt Rose stir. He propped himself on his arm and softly kissed her awake. As her eyes began to flutter he whispered, "Good morning, my beautiful Rose."

He felt her stiffen for a moment. "Simon? Where…oh." She turn a glorious shade of red.

"How do you feel this morning? Are you sore? I can run you a bath if you would like."

She shook her head as she covered a yawn. "I'm good, but I would kill for coffee."

He stood and gave her a bow. "As you wish."

"Huh…"

"What?" He grinned.

"I didn't peg you as a Princess Bride fan. But, I like it." She winked and gathered her scattered clothing.

"I'm a man with many facets," he said dramatically as he turned to leave the room.

"Holy tattoo, Batman!"

He looked over his shoulder like he would be able to see it. "You like it?"

"The wolf looks so real, I swear it could leap off your back."

"There is an interesting story behind it from when I was a Marine, I'll tell you about it one day. But it is related to all the wolfy stuff so I'll wait." He winked and left the room.

They were enjoying their first cup of coffee when the phone rang. It was Emma inviting them to brunch.

Rose looked horrified. "How did she know I was here?" she hissed.

"I have no idea how my mother knows the things she knows. I gave up trying to figure that out years ago."

"I need a shower and clothes, do I have time to go to Anna's?"

"Take your time, my mother will wait until we get there."

They enjoyed one last cup, and then he escorted her to Anna's. Even on the plantation he didn't want her going anywhere unprotected.

An hour later, Rose followed Simon into Emma's kitchen. The entire house smelled of corn bread and jambalaya. A large pot on the stove simmered and a tea towel covered the fresh baked bread. She couldn't help inhaling the scent of the amazing Cajun food, mixed with Simon's scent it was absolutely heady. Her mouth watered, she just wasn't sure if it was for the wonderful food or a taste of Simon.

Simon's gaze drifted over her, like he was drinking her in. The intensity of his hungry eyes caused a strong reaction in her body, her heart pounded, and it was hard to breathe. The slow seductive quirk of his lips put her over the edge. Her entire body swooned toward his. His fingertips brushed her face, feather-light, his touch so gentle and loving.

One hand was all it took; he wrapped her hair in his fingers and encouraged her head gently back. With excruciating slowness he lowered his lips to hers. A whisper of lips across lips, before he pulled away again. She was so hot she thought she would combust. One look, one touch, and she was ready to strip and do anything he asked. *I'm in so much trouble.* It was going to literally kill her when he ended it with her. He had said she was his girlfriend and his mate but she still didn't really understand what that meant.

As they entered the library, the entire family was gathered waiting for them. "Rose, Simon, please take a seat," Isaac called out.

Once they were seated, Isaac cleared his throat to silence the room. "I've been briefed on Rose's attack in the Quarter and the trespass of Travis Ledet onto our land. Anna also mentioned a man had followed Rose in the corner market. I believe the family is under attack and we'll need to put around the clock sentries in place and the women should be escorted when leaving the property."

Everyone was nodding in agreement. "With the sentries, do you believe the women will be safe on the property?" Simon asked.

"I don't think anyone will be able to slip through without being seen or smelled."

Simon was still uneasy after hearing of Travis's abilities but his father was rarely wrong.

"We're not sure if Rose is the prime target or Le

Beau women in general so everyone should be extra careful." Cade and Simon reached for their mates at the same time, needing the contact.

"That's really all the business we have to cover. Emma has made a feast for brunch. I hope everyone is hungry."

The family moved to the dining room and had the most elaborate brunch Rose had ever experienced. When she offered to help clean up Anna and Emma shooed her out of the kitchen.

She followed the sound of voices to the great room and sat on the couch to watch the men play a raucous game of pool.

Twenty minutes later Emma joined Rose on the couch. "So, tell me all about your family, cher."

Rose swallowed hard, she hated these questions. All of the sympathy and pity that she received with her answer about drove her mad. "My family?" Rose echoed, her heart breaking as she realized she didn't fit in Simon's family at all. Emma and Isaac were all about family. She was concerned for her son and wanting to know that Rose would be a good wife for her son, a good mother. If she had a wonderful extended family for his future children. You're supposed to learn how to be a good parent from your own mother and father, right? Well, then she was screwed.

Simon watched the color fade from Rose's cheeks. She looked to him for both rescuing and forgiveness. She felt utterly helpless and defeated. With one simple question she was beaten. She looked at the floor then glanced up at him almost helplessly and his heart turned over. She actually shrank into the cushions of the couch as if to protect herself from the question.

Simon crossed the room and sat next to her on the arm of the couch. "Rose is an orphan, Mom."

Here it comes, the pity will be first and then the rejection. No one wants an orphan with no family, no history or decent upbringing to be the mother of their grandchildren.

Anna joined them on the couch. "Rose prefers to not discuss her childhood."

Emma clucked her sympathy. "That doesn't matter, cher. When you marry Simon, you'll have all kinds of family. We'll all be your family. Shoot, you'll have more family than you know what to do with." She gathered Rose into her bosom and actually rocked her like a small child. Emma was unable to let anyone leave her presence without some mothering and in her eyes Rose had a lot of years of missed mothering.

Hold on, did she just say, when I marry Simon? Why did she say that?

"The way you grew up and the people you lived with are no never mind; it's the woman you became that's important. I just wish you would have had the love and joy little girls deserve. Lots of dolls and tea parties, birthdays and scrapbooks with all the memories. As a matter of fact, we should start a scrapbook for you right away. I'll get my camera and we'll get pictures of everything then go to the scrap book store for supplies so we can begin building fabulous memories for you." Emma zeroed in on a new project and there'd be no stopping her.

Rose could handle any challenge, but her lack of family was her kryptonite. Her reaction to others finding out about her childhood could seem unreasonable but it was something she couldn't seem to help. To change the subject, she said, "Thank you Emma, I'd like that. I hope you have lots of pictures of Simon when he was a boy. I'd love to see what he was like. I imagine he was a hand full."

Emma clapped her hands gleefully. "He was!" She raised her voice. "Isaac. Would you please bring me the family album?"

"Awww. Mom," Simon groaned "Do you have to do that to me?"

"Great idea, Emma," Isaac said cheerfully. "I bet Anna would enjoy seeing it too." He went to a large bookcase and removed a leather bound album.

"Mom! Not the pictures," Cade whined.

"I would!" Anna said.

Rose leaned in for a better look; there was a picture of a happy baby splashing excitedly in an old fashioned washtub. A few pages and he had aged to about one year old. Simon sat with his toys, waving chubby arms, hair falling into his face. Every few pages he aged a year or so. It was an incredible record of his happy childhood. It occurred to her that all of the pictures had period clothing and toys. The furniture and other things in the background were turn of the century. And they were old-fashioned black and white photos. *What the heck was that all about?*

Both Anna and Rose sat in rapt attention as Emma told story after story of Cade's and Simon's exploits.

The men sat quietly and took it like the big strong

men that they were. Groaning in agony on the inside.

Simon sent her his quick, easy grin when the photo session ended. He felt her sadness increasing with each turn of the page. She covered her sadness surprisingly well. But the level of her anxiety was becoming alarming to him.

Simon had the family Rose had always dreamt of while growing up. They loved one another, teased each other horribly, and treated each other affectionately. It surprised her how much she still craved that. She thought she'd left that behind her years ago. Now that she'd had a taste of what it was like to be a part of this family, it would destroy her when she had to go back to her lonely life in Denver.

When the album had been returned to the shelf, Rose waited for the chance to sneak from the house unnoticed. Her heart was breaking just thinking about the day she would have to pack her bags and return home. Alone. With no family. No Simon. All her life she had been an outsider. Never good enough. Never what others wanted her to be. It was a lonely place to live. The tears were threatening to spill from her eyes any second and she needed to escape.

Simon was watching her out of the corner of his eye, she was very upset and trying to hide it. Her agony tore at him. The entire situation confused him; he couldn't fix it if he didn't understand it.

Rose walked away from him, from the dream family she would never have, with a lump in her throat and tears burning behind her eyes, away from his smiling mother and his loving father. She ran from the house and rushed to reach the safety of her bedroom at

Anna's.

"Hey!" Simon came up behind her and put his arm around her shoulders. "You all right? I thought we were having fun? What happened?"

She wouldn't cry in front of him. If she had any sense she'd go home tomorrow. Maybe it would be less painful if she left now before it got any harder to leave. Before she fell even deeper in love with Simon and his family. She really didn't see any reason in prolonging the agony. She would only be here a few months and then she would have to go home. She didn't have silly hopes that Simon would fall in love with her and ask her to marry him. Men like him didn't marry women like her. Better to rip the Band-Aid off quickly.

Rose shrugged Simon off and walked more quickly, practically running down the hall. It was a cowardly thing to do, but she had to get away before the tears started. She didn't owe him an explanation. Hell, she didn't know how to explain it. What she did know was that if she spent one more minute with him she'd be sobbing on his shoulder. The door had barely closed and the lock turned when Simon crashed into it.

"Rose, baby, please talk to me. Whatever it is, let me make it better." The desperation in his voice was growing.

Rose lay on the bed with her face buried in the pillow weeping as her heart shattered.

Hearing her sobs and feeling her heart break was too much. Taking a step back he rammed the door knocking it off its hinges. He hadn't even realized what he was doing until he was standing on the other side of the door.

Simon: Le Beau Brothers

Rose screamed and bolted from the bed.

In two steps Simon was on her. He grabbed her up in his arms, burying his face in her neck. His entire body was shaking so badly he wasn't able to stand. With a slight turn of their bodies, he tumbled them to the bed.

The family came running as they heard the crash of the door from across the yard to find Rose wrapped in Simon's arms weeping heart-wrenching tears.

Isaac waved everyone away. They needed privacy. He would speak with Simon once everyone settled down.

It was a long time before Rose quieted. Simon wanted to get her tissues but he was terrified of letting go of her. A few minutes later she lifted her head. Her mascara ran down her face, her nose and eyes were red, she'd never been more beautiful to him.

"Will you please tell me what's wrong? Did I do or say something?" His wolf was howling in agony feeling its mate's pain.

"I can't stay here, Simon. I don't belong. I'm not part of the family. If I stay any longer, my heart will shatter when I need to go back to Denver. You're having fun now but you're going to get bored with me like the others. I need to leave now, before it's too late."

"NO!" It came out as a sharp command. His wolf leapt to the surface. He struggled to soften his tone. "Please don't leave me, Rose. I'm begging you. Please stay." His voice broke and a tear ran down his cheek

At that she lifted her head and looked at him. "Why? Why is it so important to you that I stay?" This didn't make sense to her, yes, she had slept with him, but that didn't mean much to men.

"You may not believe me but I love you, baby. You're my mate, there is literally no other woman for me."

"Everyone keeps calling me your mate. What the hell does that even mean?" She was frustrated now.

"For every shifter there is only one woman, one mate. You search all your life for the special woman meant for only you. When a shifter is born, he has half a soul, his mate has the other half. There's a mating ritual that binds the two pieces of the soul together. Once a shifter finds his mate, she's everything to him. He has no interest in any other woman, no desire for any other woman. You are literally my other half, my everything. I'll never leave you, never cheat on you. I only want to protect you, love you, and make you happy."

She sighed. "That sounds like the perfect fairy tale. How can you be so sure I'm your mate? You could be with me for a while and then decide someone else is your mate."

He shook his head. "There are specific signs. You'll be unnaturally drawn to the person and once you are close enough you will smell the most delicious scent you've ever smelled."

Her head came up and she started listening intently.

"Then when you hear her voice it's like the world becomes brighter, more colorful. I can't even begin to describe it properly. Finally, the unmistakable sign is you'll be able to talk telepathically to your mate."

"And you've had all these signs?"

"Yes, I'm sure you have too. When I'm near you do you smell anything special?"

She looked at the floor again, afraid to say it in case it wasn't real.

He bent way down so he could force her to look at him. "Rose?"

"Yes, I smell fresh linen, like freshly washed sheets," she whispered.

I smell the most exquisite combination of coffee and cinnamon rolls. He grinned and waited for her to react to hearing him telepathically.

She smiled, as she looked him in the eye. "I smell like breakfast?" She laughed.

"The best breakfast in the world."

"So, you really can't ever leave me?"

"Nope, I wouldn't want to anyway. You're beautiful and the most amazing woman I've ever met. You're everything to me, baby. I love you so much, it hurts."

"But what happens if you don't do this mating ritual you mentioned?"

"Then our souls won't be complete, and you won't get your wolf soul and your magic."

"Back up the bus. What wolf soul and magic?"

"When we do the ritual, you'll receive a wolf soul and be able to shift like me. You also get magic so you can put on clothes with a thought, heal and move super fast. Stuff like that."

"That's the special abilities you talked about at the diner right?"

"Exactly." He was beginning to breathe easier and

the knot in his stomach eased.

"What's the ritual?"

"First there is the request. I'll ask you formally if you'll give yourself to me to make me complete. I ask you, will you give yourself, body and soul, to complete this man and his wolf? Will you unite your life with mine, bond your future with mine, and merge your half of our soul to mine, and in doing so complete the mating ritual?

"The second part is your formal response, which is: I will give myself, body and soul, to complete you as a man and a wolf. I will unite my life with yours, bond my future to yours, and merge my half of our soul with yours. I will complete the mating ritual with you.

"Then as we join our bodies together and while we make love, I make my vow to you, which is: I claim you as my mate. I belong to you as you belong to me. I give you my heart and my body. I will protect you with my life. I give you all I am. I share my half of our soul to complete you. I share my magic with you. I beseech the great Luna Goddess to bless you and your wolf guardian. You are my mate to cherish today and for all time. I claim you as my mate.

"At the part where I say I share my magic with you, I bite you right here, where your neck and shoulder meet. But don't worry, I'm told it isn't painful and you'll enjoy it. Then you say those same words to me and bite me in the same manner. That's the complete ritual."

"You're not playin' me? That actually works?"

"Yes, it does, if you don't believe me ask Anna."

She gasped. "She did it? She is a shifter too?" She

144

jumped up and ran to ask Anna. She found her in the kitchen. "Anna, did you do the ritual?"

Simon leaned against the kitchen island chuckling at the look on Anna's face.

Anna looked from Rose to Simon and back again. She turned to Simon before she responded to Rose. "Did you explain it all to her?"

"Yes, I told her about the entire ritual."

"CADE!" she called.

He came from the great room. "Cher? Is something wrong?"

She turned to Rose. "Yes, I have done the ritual with Cade."

"So, you can shift and have magic and stuff?"

"Yes, and there is something else you both need to know. Rose, you'll regress in age until you look like you did when you were about twenty five." She raised an eyebrow at Cade and suddenly she looked twenty five again.

Rose's hand flew to her mouth and her eyes became huge. She reached for a bar stool and sat.

"Are you okay?"

"Yeah, just give me a minute."

While she was recovering, Cade tapped Simon on the shoulder. "We all need to talk about the conversion. When she's ready, come into the great room." He and Anna left them to talk in the kitchen.

"Rose, are you sure you're okay? You look really pale."

"I just need to wrap my head around seeing my best friend do that before my eyes." She waved her hand around. "So, I'll do that too. Look all…young again."

"Yes." He hesitated. "Um, Rose?"

She gave him a questioning look.

"Please tell me you weren't a skinny stick of a woman at twenty five. I mean I'll love you no matter what, but damn girl, I like your soft curves."

Her eyebrows went up and she laughed at his pained expression. "No, Simon, I've always been plus sized."

"Thank Goddess."

She shook her head at him. "Let's find out what other bombs they are going to drop on me today."

Once everyone was settled in the great room, Cade look them both in the eyes. "After the ritual, within a few minutes, Rose will begin to regress. Simon, there won't be much you can do but stay with her and keep your mouth shut."

Anna took her friend's hand. "It's not terribly painful. Your body will go through changes to anti-age for lack of a better word. Your skin will tighten, wrinkles will smooth out, and everything turns back the clock, even your ovaries. That's why I can have a baby again." She grinned and rubbed her tummy. "My best advice is to watch a Lamaze video with me and practice breathing before you do the ritual. It'll help you a lot."

"Is there a time limit we need to do the ritual by?" she asked.

Cade answered for Simon. "No, but the longer you wait, the harder it is on Simon."

Simon growled at Cade. He didn't want anyone pressuring his mate.

"Cool it, Cujo. I need to know the truth." She

looked to Anna. "Want to watch a video with me this afternoon?"

"I'd love to. I even have popcorn," she said happily.

Chapter 11

Rose Moves In

How could the past two weeks have been any more perfect?

Oh, wait, they couldn't. He smiled as he imagined waking next to Rose every morning in his bed.

Rose had finally agreed to move her belongings from Anna's house to his. Both his wolf's soul and the man thanked Goddess for this woman. She was a gift more precious than he deserved but he was honored that he'd been blessed with her as his mate.

He paced the deck as she unpacked. When he'd tried to help she'd swatted him and shooed him away. He didn't understand what was taking so long. She only had a few suitcases of clothes.

A faint scent of panic struck him the moment he passed the screen door. Her anxiety caused his own to spike. Had Travis come back for her?

"Rose?" No answer. "Rose!" he yelled as he burst through the door, sending bits of doorjamb flying in all directions. "Rose? Where are you?" Hers was the only scent in the house, so what had caused her to panic?

Then he heard her cursing in the walk in closet.

"I'm trying to fix the closet rod, it fell as I was hanging my clothes!" she yelled back. "The rod let loose on one end and all of my clothes are trying to slide off."

He ran to help her, relieved there was no threat lurking. *Why did I build the bedrooms way back here?* He snarled as he rushed through the house.

A thud sounded, followed by a louder curse and low whimper. As he entered the bedroom, he saw Rose struggling to push one end of the closet rod back into place while blood trickled to her elbow.

He took the sagging rod from her. "There is a length of 2x4 in the coat closet by the back door, could you get that?" She ran to get it and he wedged it under the rod. "I'll get a new bracket from the hardware store later and fix it properly," waving toward the board, "that should hold for now. Are you all right?" he asked as he tried to assess her injury.

"I'm fine. The rod just slipped and scraped down my arm." She raised it for him to see.

Over the past two weeks Simon had dedicated himself to courting Rose. It had been a slow process convincing her she was the only woman in the world for him. But, persistence paid off. She now believed he thought she was beautiful, sexy, and he'd never want anyone else. And now he had her living in his home, life was good.

Simon set her coffee in front of her as they relaxed to plan their day. "Cher, would you like to go dancing tonight?"

"There's a club around here?" Her brows disappeared into the hair across her forehead.

"My cousin Julia has a place in the bayou, you can only get to it by boat. She jokingly named it the Backwater to annoy her parents. She has a live band on

Saturday nights. I'm told the music is usually pretty good."

"Sounds like fun. What time should I be ready?"

"We can go after dinner, whenever we're ready."

"Okay, I better get moving. I promised to help Anna paint the baby's room today." She gave him a kiss on the cheek and left with her coffee.

This new comfortable relationship feels like we're a mated couple, he mused. *I like it.*

Rose placed the last of the dinner dishes in the washer when she felt the air behind her stir. Without turning her head, she knew it was Simon. She felt his presence like a tangible touch.

She looked at him over her shoulder. His blue eyes seared her with heat. The intensity of his stare made her shiver. Lifting one hand, he laid his fingers against the blush of her cheek. Then he wrapped his arms around her from behind. He buried his nose in her hair and let his wolf rumble in satisfaction. "I'm ready to show you off at Julia's whenever you are ready to go."

"Let me check my face and hair. It'll only take a minute." She returned a few minutes later looking amazing.

Her hair was pulled back in a fashionable messy bun. A single strand was left loose to fall down the side of her face to the tip of her breast. He longed to follow that strand to its destination, scrape his teeth against her nipple and inhale her precious scent.

She was without a doubt the most beautiful creature he'd ever seen in his life. Rose placed her arms around his neck, and he relished how her warmth seeped into his body.

"I may have to change my mind, you look too good, and I'll be forced to kill some idiot who tries to dance with you."

She rolled her eyes at him and grabbed her purse. "Come on, Romeo, I'm ready for a boat ride and a turn around the dance floor."

Simon held her hand as she got into the boat then jumped in and revved the motor. "I'll go slow so I don't mess up your gorgeous hair." He winked.

She blew him a kiss and fluffed her hair dramatically.

Even going slow it only took twenty minutes to reach the pier serving the bar. He already heard the music and boisterous patrons. He cut the motor and helped her exit safely; boats weren't designed for high heels.

Rose looked up and down the line of boat slips and shoreline. "Where's her sign?"

"She doesn't have one. We'd rather random humans didn't wonder in. Mates are more than welcome, but the occasional human to happen upon the bar isn't very well received."

He led her to an open table. "I'll get us drinks, would you like wine or a whiskey Coke?"

"A whiskey Coke sounds great." Her eyes were bright with excitement as she checked out the crowd.

He squeezed into an open spot at the bar and waved his cousin over. "Julia! How are you, cher?"

"Oh, mon dieu! Simon, it's so good to see you. I heard you found your mate."

"I did." He gestured to their table. "Rose is seated right there, stop over if you get a break."

"Oh, elle est de toute beauté. You're a lucky man, cuz."

"Don't I know it." He grinned. "Can I get a Whiskey Coke and a beer?"

"Oui."

He turned his back to the bar to check on Rose. Simon's breath caught as she unconsciously moistened her lip with the tip of her pink tongue. That mouth was made for sin, with its plush lower lip. He imagined her mouth doing wicked things to a certain part of his anatomy. Blood thrummed in his veins. Simon turned to inconspicuously adjust himself, his faded jeans were suddenly way too tight. Her intoxicating scent of coffee and cinnamon rolls licked at his groin even from across the room. He wanted to rub himself all over her, saturating her with his scent whenever they were in public. His wolf wouldn't be satisfied until they were mated.

Gazing at her across the room his blood surged, he imagined her naked on his bed, her thighs parted in invitation. He lowered his head and tasted her passion. Loving her long into the night, her excited cries entwining with his hoarse groans as they made the bed shudder and shake. He shook his head. He really needed to get control of his randy thoughts. This was date night and he would show her a good time away from his bed for once. *Down boy, he snarled at his wolf.* When he glanced at her again she was snickering and shaking her head at him. He must be imagining loudly.

"Here you go, no charge, and congratulations, Simon." Julia rapped her knuckles on the bar top before she turned her attention to making another customer's drink. She was very busy, so he left her to it. He'd barely taken his seat when the band took the stage for another set. He stood and held his hand out to Rose. "May I have this dance?"

"Why, yes, you may," she said, back playing along.

Simon held her close enough to see the sparkles in her blue eyes. He loved the way her gaze lit up when she was happy. But his wolf itched to see her eyes dazed with passion as he made love to her, and then sated and sleepy afterwards. For now holding her on the dance floor would do. Rose's intoxicating fragrance surrounded him, teasing his senses. He was in heaven.

He cupped her cheek with a large, warm palm. "I'm so happy you moved into our house, Rose. Having you in my arms makes me the luckiest man in the world." The moment she agreed to move to his house he'd called it *their* home. His glowing blue eyes regarded her with a tenderness that made her breath hitch.

She tightened her arms around his neck, urging his face closer to hers. "I didn't want to go back to Anna's, to an empty bed anymore," she told him. "If you really plan to have me as your mate, it only made sense."

"Just say the word and I'm yours completely. Forever." He smiled, then dipped his head, kissed her deeply and nuzzled her.

She felt his breath on her neck as he breathed her in. He really liked doing that. Shivers ran up her spine when she felt him gently kiss where he said he would put his mating mark. Playing the vixen, she rubbed her body against his.

Over the past weeks, his sincere, quiet assurances, the way he gazed into her eyes as if she were the only woman in the world, had triggered a daring side she never knew she possessed. Her lace bra felt too restrictive against her sensitive, erect nipples as her actions created an intense stimulation. A pleasant ache began pulsing between her legs. From the passionate interest in his eyes, she knew he smelled her arousal.

Lowering his head, he kissed her again. She closed her eyes, relishing the sweetness of his tender kiss.

"You," he dragged in a deep breath, as if it took great effort to control himself, "are the most beautiful woman I've ever seen. You're what I've always imagined the perfect woman to be. How did I get so lucky?"

She touched his cheek, caressing with her thumb. He smiled then turned his head to catch her thumb in his mouth and suckle it.

Desire flared in her veins. The air fled her lungs at his sheer sexual intensity. He wrapped a strand of her silky hair around his finger and drew her close.

"A small preview," he murmured as his eyes burned brighter. His body was so damned hard he was afraid of taking a step, afraid of moving. He couldn't ever remember having such a raging hard-on or such a painful need to relieve it.

He led her to their table where they could watch the band and cool off. If he didn't calm his libido he might set this bar ablaze with his intense need. He hoped Rose would agree to be his mate soon, his wolf was getting more feral by the day. "I'm going to get another beer would you like another drink?"

"Just a Coke this time."

The moment he left the table she felt a familiar prickling sensation crawl up her neck. Someone was watching her. A rancid breath scorched her skin right before she heard a familiar voice behind her. It dragged her back to the abandoned store with the muggers.

She flew to her feet sending her chair crashing to the floor. Spinning to defend herself, she found an empty space. There was no one there. Her gaze darted around the bar, searching for his face. *How could he just disappear?*

Simon flew to her side, "Babe, what is it?"

"Him. Travis. He was behind me."

"Guard her!" He ordered the men nearest her. A massive snarl erupted as he shifted in the middle of the bar. Simon was able to transform into a wolf the size of a Mastiff. He had a blond coat with a multitude of colors running through it, black, blond, even milk chocolate. Expressive almond-shaped, sky blue eyes normally sparkled behind long lush lashes that any woman would kill for. Today they looked dangerous. His wolf had a muscular frame, and a walk that resembled more of a prowl than anything else. Shifters senses were far more acute than humans. Even in human form they had a heightened senses of smell, hearing, and vision. But as a wolf, few could track better than Simon.

The crowd moved out of his way like a flock of sheep avoiding a predator. Frantically he searched for the scent he needed. He couldn't find the tiniest whiff of Travis. Other shifters joined his search as it spilled onto the grounds surrounding the bar. Nothing.

Jason Ledet walked to Simon's side and waited for him to shift. "You won't find him that way."

"Why not?" Simon growled savagely.

"He can block his and anyone else's scent he chooses. You need to search for a complete lack of scent. That is the clue to where he's been."

Simon was so worked up he was panting. He took one last look into the dense forest then returned to Rose.

He held out his hand to her. "Sweetheart, we should go. I no longer feel you are safe here."

"All right." Without argument she left with him. She wouldn't say it in front of all these strangers, but she didn't think she was safe either.

Simon seated Rose next to him in the rear of the boat going home. He and his wolf needed to keep her close and she seemed to want it as well.

Rose dug through her purse for her Chapstick, that's when she realized something was missing. "I think he stole my wallet."

Simon idled the motor and reached for her purse. One sniff and he knew she was right, no scent at all. Travis had touched it. "What was in it?" he asked warily.

"My drivers license, credit cards, all the normal stuff."

"He has your Denver address. I'm sorry, baby, I wanted to give you more time before I asked this of you. But, it's not safe for you there anymore. Are you willing to move permanently to our home?"

"You really think he would go all the way to Denver?"

"He's insane, he doesn't do rational things. Yes, he would go there if he thought you were there."

She sighed. "Then I guess I better pack my things and move."

"I can call Etienne. He has people in Denver. They'll pack your belongings and escort them to you. As long as your household is guarded he won't be able to try anything. I wouldn't put it past him to boobie trap boxes to harm you."

"I really don't like anyone digging in my stuff."

Laughing, he said, "I know. I have first hand experience with being denied touching your stuff when you moved from Anna's."

"Sorry about that, old habits you know. If you think its best, I'll get over it."

He let out a long breath. "Great, I'll feel much better after I call Et and put his men on the job."

She waited for him on the dock while he secured the boat in the slip. She didn't feel safe even walking across the lawn to his home.

Once inside, he locked the door. She kissed him lightly. "I'm going to wash my face and get out of these heels." She looked him directly in the eye as she unzipped her skirt and let it drop to the floor as she left him in the kitchen wearing, nothing but a thong and four-inch heels from the waist down.

Simon was thrilled with the sexy woman Rose had blossomed into. With a look or a gesture she could set him on fire. *Well, two could play at that game.* But first he had a call to make.

"Hello?"

"Hello, Etienne, this is Simon Le beau."

"Simon, it's a pleasure to hear from you, how is the lovely Rose?"

"She becomes more beautiful everyday. I'm calling because I need your assistance on her behalf."

"What can I do for her?"

"The rogue shifter Travis is still stalking her and tonight he stole her wallet from her purse. He now has her personal information about her home in Denver. We need to have her apartment packed and moved here to our home at once. I don't trust letting her things out of sight, so I'd like the moving van ushered here."

"I agree, that mutt is a menace and utterly insane. He could try anything. Her items should never go unguarded. Consider it done, and please give my friend a kiss on the cheek for me."

"Thank you, Et, I appreciate the assist more than you know."

He ended the call and proceeded with Operation Payback Rose.

Simon: Le Beau Brothers

She found Simon sitting on the kitchen counter, eating ice cream from the carton. Leather jacket and boots still on, it looked like he had gone straight to the freezer when they got back.

Slowly he spooned the frozen treat into his mouth, eyes locked on her, strong throat muscles working as he wrapped his tongue around the spoon and then swallowed.

Transfixed by the sight, she stopped at the door. This man made eating ice cream look wonderfully sinful.

Never taking his eyes from hers, his tongue slowly stroked a drop off the spoon. It curled around the backside to get every bit of sweetness.

His gaze flicked to her clinching fists then he raised his nose and sniffed deeply capturing her rich scent of arousal. The rumble from his chest caused moisture to seep onto her clenched thighs. A growl of appreciation erupted from his throat as his wolf came into his eyes.

Simon ran his tongue over his lips, then he brought another spoonful of ice cream to his mouth and slid it in. Rose's nipples beaded to stiff peaks and her toes curled.

"I love your scent. I could pick you out of a thousand women, blindfolded. You're so perfectly unique."

He gave a seductive smile and gestured with the spoon. "Want some?"

"Oh, yeah, but not the ice cream."

He crooked a finger at her, his smile sexy and enticing. "Come here, cher."

She sashayed to him, wedged his thighs further apart and pressed her hips into him. Her hands reached under his chin, tugged down the zipper of his jacket. She was on tiptoe trying to push the leather from his shoulders, the man was too tall sometimes.

He slid off the counter and let her tear it off him. "I like when you take control."

Next she removed his shirt. She eyed his jeans, slid her fingers half way in and used them to lead him to the bedroom.

Stopping next to the bed the whisper of his zipper was the only sound in the room as she stripped his jeans down his legs. His knees began to shake. "Cher," he said, taking her hands. "It's my turn."

He slid his palms under the hem of her sweater and slowly pushed it up. Rose lifted her arms so he could pull it over her head. He tossed it aside and with two fingers popped the clasp of her bra. The lacy scrap fell free, releasing her breasts to his gaze.

She ran her hands up his chest under his T-shirt. A jolt of exquisite pleasure shot through him as she found a nipple and circled it, pinched it. Pushing the shirt higher, he helped her pull it over his head.

With his hands freed, he tangled them in her hair and kissed her senseless.

"Boots?" she breathed huskily.

"Yes, please."

Wearing only her heels and thong, she bent down and unlaced them, slowly. She made it into a strip tease as she tossed each boot and then his pants across the room. Every move caused her breasts to sway. His mouth salivated watching her strip him bare. He was naked and very erect.

With a sexy wiggle of her hips, she began her own strip tease as she tucked her thumbs under her thong's elastic and slowly worked them down her legs and over her heels. She brazenly offered the panties to him, which he gleefully accepted. Crushing them to his nose he inhaled. Her scent had his eyes rolling in his head and his erection twitching.

She was watching him as she rolled her nipples when he opened his eyes. His heart stuttered to a stop.

"On the bed?" she questioned when he remained frozen in place.

Coming to his senses, he leapt to the bed and flung himself down on his back. He wore nothing but a grin as he drank her in.

He reached down and stroked himself knowing it was a real turn on for her to watch. "Make love to me, mon coeur." His outstretched hand invited her to join him.

Nibbling her fingernail, she ran her gaze over him from head to toe, one last time. Bracing her hands on his strong thighs, she leaned forward and ran her tongue over his bare skin, feeling him quiver. She licked a trail from his throat to his left pec, her tongue swirling around one small brown nipple, then she lightly nipped, enjoying his rumbling groan. She flicked it with her tongue, then licked her way down his rippling stomach, running her tongue along each valley. She followed the enticing line of hair trailing lower and had almost reached her goal.

He slid his hands into her hair and drew her back to his lips. Captured her mouth with his own. Simon licked the inside of her mouth, stroking his tongue slowly as she moaned and squirmed. The long, lingering kiss set her on fire.

Both his human soul and wolf soul craved this. They craved her. He wrapped one arm around her and flipped them both so he was on top. Rose threw back her head as Simon nudged her legs apart. His ragged breath scorched her thighs.

She ran her fingers down his smooth cheek to his lower lip. He nipped them playfully. She watched him as he nudged her legs farther and took her into his mouth. She moaned in pleasure as her legs quivered. Seeking to sooth her aching nipples, she stroked them.

Simon lifted his head and regarded her, his intent gaze glowing. "Touch yourself, Rose. I want you soaked and ready for me when I make love to you. I'm going to make you burn, make you scream. I want to taste your climax on my tongue." He gave a wicked grin. "And that's just the beginning."

He devoured her. There was no other word for it. He slowly swirled his tongue over her clit as his fingers squeezed and kneaded her ass. Very lightly, he bit. She screamed.

He licked and teased until her head spun. Her body wound tighter as he stroked his tongue faster and harder until she could take it no longer. And then he gave one last flick, and she shattered. Screaming, her body convulsed with an explosive orgasm He turned her body inside out by his masterful tongue and touch.

He gently soothed her with tiny kisses, until the last spasm faded and she lay limp and panting.

Simon rumbled at the sound of her pleasure, at the taste of it. There was nothing sweeter than hearing the screams of a mate climaxing. Sitting back, he wiped his mouth with the back of his hand.

"I love you," she breathed.

The wolf in him howled in satisfaction. Not only had they satisfied their mate, but she had declared her love for them.

He kissed his way up her body slowly until he covered her skin with his own. She looked at him with affection shining brightly in the blue depths of her eyes. He braced himself above her, leaving space between their bodies. He took her hand into his and led it to his throbbing erection.

His short, crisp hairs teased her fingers. He growled deep in his throat as she wrapped her fist around the hard length of him. The man was large and he was already wet and straining.

Threading his fingers in her hair, he kissed her passionately while she stroked him.

"That is what you do to me, Rose. All it takes is a thought and I'm hard as a rock for you. I love you with all my heart."

He positioned himself at her core. "Guide me, Rose."

She held him while he slid into her slick folds feeling their bodies join.

He lingered over her, loving her, he wanted this first time together living under the same roof declaring their love to be special. Taking his time as he slid in to the hilt. Then he withdrew, and set a slow exquisite pace.

Rose's fingers dug into his shoulder muscles, her gaze fierce with a longing as deep as his own as she thrust her hips upward. "I want you, Simon, hard and furious," she pleaded.

Raising, Simon withdrew slightly. Then he surged forward. Dark blond hairs at his groin nestled against her exquisite mound.

She hooked her legs around his waist drawing him deeper. He obeyed her and began to thrust harder. Hard and fast. He angled his thrusts, hitting a particularly sensitive spot. She cried out. Her body felt like it shattered into a thousand pieces.

Simon shouted as he joined her in his own hot release. He collapsed atop her, his heavy weight pinning her. Then he rolled to the side not wanting to crush her. Their harsh breathing was loud in the silence of the room.

The next morning, Rose woke confused. She didn't recognize where she was for a second. Then she fell back into her pillow with a knowing grin. She laughed at herself. She didn't remember falling asleep or even pulling up the covers. When had she become this person?

After her shower, she went searching for Simon and coffee, rounded the corner into the kitchen. A naked man stood at the stove, frying bacon. *Holy mother, what an ass!*

He turned his head and offered a lazy grin. "Morning, cher. Want some breakfast?"

"Frying bacon in the nude? Are you nuts?"

"Adventurous. I like to think of myself as adventurous."

Lordy, Simon in jeans and T-shirt was heart stopping. But naked Simon fried all her circuits. Sculpted muscles reigned supreme. A glorious landscape of muscle framed his back, dipping down to his taut…Oh yeah. Nothing like a man with a very firm ass. She was tempted to sink her teeth into it.

As he started to turn, she had second thoughts about him sitting at the table naked. "Please, put some clothes on."

He plucked an apron off a hook near the stove and tied it around his waist, leaving his very fine ass exposed to her hungry eyes.

Two warm hands cupped her cheeks, then he ran a thumb over her bottom lip. A shiver coursed down her spine. "You're very beautiful this morning, as always."

Her eyes closed as his mouth descended on hers. His gentle, sweet kiss, simmered with passion. Rose inhaled his clean fresh linen scent, arousal flooding her. When he drew away, disappointment stabbed her.

Something else stabbed at her as well, hard and prodding. Simon grinned proudly, "Sorry. My general condition when I'm around you. I can't help but get turned on."

She shook her head at his antics.

They enjoyed their breakfast and another cup of coffee. He was cleaning the frying pan when he looked over his shoulder. "Stefan needs me to join him on a site today so I'll be gone for a few hours."

"Oh, okay. I'm sure I'll find something to keep me busy. I thought I'd plan us a special night tonight." She glanced at him out of the corner of her eye.

"What are you up to, Rose?"

"I'm ready, Simon."

"Do you mean…?"

"Yes, tonight I'm claiming you as my mate." She laughed as he snatched her from the chair and swung her around in a circle.

"You mean it? Really?"

"Yes. I do. And I wanted to make a special dinner for us, so I'm going to ask Anna if she wants to go to the store with me."

"All right but take Marcus or Cade with you, I don't want you out alone. By the way, Etienne has his men taking care of your apartment."

"Thank you, I'll feel better once everything is here. And, if I can't get one of them to join us, I'll make due with what ever is in the house, okay?"

"Thank you. I can't leave you if I'll be worried. Look at the time, I need to hurry." He kissed her passionately one last time and ran to get dressed.

Chapter 12

Danger comes calling

Rose had butterflies gathering in her stomach, tonight was the night everything would change. She was on her way to the corner store with Anna and Marcus, grocery list in hand.

Marcus looked each of his little sisters in the eyes. "I'll remain just outside the door, keeping watch. If anything looks or smells wrong call out. Travis needs to be stopped," he growled.

His smoky gray eyes turn liquid silver as his wolf jumped to the forefront. People only saw what Marcus wanted them to see, a well dressed businessman. What they didn't see until it was too late was the merciless killer he hid so well behind his very cultivated easy going demeanor.

Rose scanned the aisles searching for the perfect ingredients for her special dinner. As she studied a display of steaks, her skin began to crawl and the hair on the back of her neck rose. She spun on her heel to catch Dark Hair glaring before he rushed into the back receiving dock. "Marcus!"

The entrance door slammed open, crashing into the wall followed by a hair-raising snarl. "Where?" He demanded in a guttural growl as his eyes searched the store.

"Through there." She pointed.

"Russell, protect them." He ordered as he disappeared into the dark back room.

Rose could hardly breathe as she waited for Marcus to return. A few minutes passed before Marcus walked through the shattered front door. A dangerous glower on his face.

"Did you get him?" Anna asked.

"No. I searched the grounds as well as the perimeter. Are you ladies finished?"

"Ye..Yes, I can make due with what I have." Rose didn't want to be anywhere near Dark Hair. She trembled all the way home, *will they ever stop stalking me*?

"Do you want me to stay with you?" Anna asked once the bags were unloaded in Simon's kitchen.

She hugged her best friend then rubbed her baby bump. "No. I'll be fine now that we're home. You have things to do." She knew Anna had plans to shop for a crib today with Emma.

"If you are absolutely sure," she asked a bit more sternly.

"Absolutely, now shoo." She nudged her toward the door.

Two hours later, she was finalizing her meal plan and gathering recipes when she heard the cry of an injured animal. It sounded close to the house. Two things Rose could never deny, a crying baby and an injured animal. She had seen too much neglect and abuse growing up.

Squinting she searched the area from the safety of the back door. She couldn't see the poor creature. Stepping onto the deck she listened intently. The pain filled whimper came from her left near the edge of the yard where the low shrubbery began. She took a few steps that direction trying to locate the animal within the tangle of roots and limbs.

The pitiful cries drew her from the deck to within a few feet of the dense shrubs. She craned her neck trying to see into the shadowy depths. One final step brought her within arms length of the largest, thickest ground cover and shrubbery.

A hand clamped over her mouth as another yanked her into the tree cover.

She tried to bite the hand but it held her too tightly. Then she frantically kicked at her attacker's shins with her heel. She heard a grunt. Bull's eye! Direct hit. Leaning forward as far as she could, she slammed her head back. All that did was give her a screaming headache when she connected with a solid chest instead of the jaw she'd hoped for.

The last thing she would remember was an angry snarl rumbling from the chest that held her. Then everything went black.

Ah, my head is splitting. She rubbed her temples to alleviate the throb. *What's jabbing me?* She wondered as she opened her eyes. Panic immediately gripped her. Heart racing she rolled left. All that did was introduce her forehead to the wall. "Ow!" She rubbed the rising bump then rolled the other direction trying to identify where she was.

Her skin prickled as she had the all too familiar sensation of being watched. Scanning the room she squinted to see into the far corner, which was heavily shadowed. An enormous man stood from a chair, staring at her. Rose scrambled as far as the handcuffs would let her, and pressed herself into the wall. He smelled nasty and looked even worse. Her heart stopped as she saw the crazed look that shone in his eyes.

She couldn't look away from the intensity of his glare, no matter how hard she tried, or how much she wanted to.

His ragged dirty hair and clothes made him appear even more intimidating—that and the scowl on his grime smeared face. Panic sent her pulse into orbit. Simon was gone and didn't know she'd been taken. No one knew she was even missing! She was on her own and this man definitely meant her harm.

Recognition dawned. It was Travis, the insane shifter. He was so dirty she hadn't recognized him at first.

He's dragged me off somewhere.

I'm going to die.

"It was very accommodating of Simon, to leave you unprotected." Drool hung at the corner of his mouth.

Her mind raced, *wildlife shows always say to not show fear* she thought, so she tried indignation. "It's rude to stare," she made sure her voice remained steady.

"You'll keep a civil tongue, mate." His voice was a deep, thunderous rumble that told her that this guy didn't play around…

Okay, try another tactic. "I'm not your mate. Who are you?" she countered sweetly.

"Travis. And you are my mate if I say you are." He spoke through clenched teeth. A large vein ticked on his forehead.

She's eying me like I'm the bad guy, I'm not a bad guy. Travis deluded himself. *They want me to kill her but she'd make a fine mate for me. I'll keep the others off her and test her survival skills. If she lasts a few days out here, she's worthy of me and I just might keep her. I could live with her in a cabin deep in the swamp where the Le Beaus would never find us... Finally happy. I deserve to be happy. I don't want money, I want a mate.* His fractured mind ranted incessantly.

"Simon's going to rip your throat out!" She glared at him. "He'll never stop until you're a mangy rug on his floor."

He clamped his jaw and his lip curled back in a sneer. Then stepped toward her menacingly.

She shrieked. High pitched, like an icepick to his eardrum shrieks.

He snapped his hand forward and slapped her hard. "Stop that noise!"

She glared at him and shrieked louder. Her temper tended to get her into trouble.

"Enough!" He drew his fist back like he was going to slug her.

She silenced. Her eyes fixed on him defiantly.
Then a devious look passed over her face. She opened
her mouth and began to sing at the top of her lungs, that
annoying children's song. What was that lamb chop
song called? Oh yeah, The Song That Never Ends.
"This is the song that never ends, yes it goes on and on
my friend…."

Come to find out, that song never ends.

Ever.

He clamped his hands over his ears. "Stop singing
that."

"I'll make a deal with you. Take the cuffs off and
I stop singing."

He hesitated and she started singing again. He
immediately took the deal. She'd stop singing, and he'd
take the cuffs off, there was nowhere for her to go
anyway so it was no skin off his nose.

She rubbed her sore wrists once the cuffs were
removed. She'd been unconscious long enough to need
the powder room. Stealing her resolve she swung her
legs off the bed to stand. Ready for anything, there was
no telling how *nut job* would react to movement.

"Where do you think you're going?" He jabbed
his finger in her face, "I didn't give you permission to
get off the bed."

Rose had always reacted badly to being jabbed at,
her horrible, abusive foster father had done that to her.
A lot. She would NEVER be a victim again. She glared
up from her place on the bed and growled, "move it or
lose it."

He looked startled.

She snapped her teeth at his finger catching the tip

before he pulled back.

"You bit me!" he roared as he wrapped his hands around her neck.

Shit, shouldn't have done that. She thought too late. Lack of oxygen caused an odd ringing in her ears. Her heart racing, she couldn't catch her breath. Oh, God this was it.

Simon bounded up the back stairs, he couldn't wait to hold his mate in his arms. "Rose, I'm home." Silence greeted him. He searched every inch of the house, with each empty room his panic grew. *Rose? Where are you, baby?* She didn't answer his telepathic call. Rose was gone. Disbelief racked him. *Why would she leave? She accepted me this morning. This is our ritual night.* It made zero sense, she had to be here somewhere.

He snatched his cell phone from his pocket. "Anna, is Rose with you?"

"No, I left her at your house after we got home from the grocery store."

"Did she mention needing to go anywhere else?"

"She was too scared to go anywhere after Dark Hair showed up at the store."

"WHAT! What happened? Did he touch her?" The plastic casing of the phone cracked in his grip.

"No, he ran out the back. Marcus went after him but he got away."

"Would you call Stefan and Marcus, make sure she isn't with them? I'll call Dad and Mom."

"You got it," he heard a click and dialed his

parents. They hadn't seen her all day. With his heart hammering against his ribs he paced as he waited to hear from Anna.

His phone didn't have the chance to finish its first ring. "Did you find her?"

"No, hun. They haven't seen her either. I told them to meet us at your parent's. Simon don't take off on your own, we need to keep level heads and organize a search party."

Helpless frustration felt like a knife piercing his heart. He flew out the door and raced to the main house. Fear had him coated in sweat as he was forced to wait for everyone to gather. It felt like an eternity.

Worried murmurs and cursing began to fill the room.

He couldn't stand it. He had turned toward the exit when a hand gently touched his arm.

"Simon," Emma pleaded. "Please. You need to wait for the boys. You know better than to go after a predator blind without backup."

"You can't trespass on other packs' property, son. Give us time to notify the alphas. They will help search for her. If you encroach on their territory without permission the situation will only get worse," Isaac reasoned.

He snarled but capitulated.

Isaac signaled Emma for privacy. "Anna would you help me with a few things?" Emma asked.

He waited until Emma and Anna left the room before addressing Simon and Cade. "If your mother knew the threat level Travis and his crew presented, neither of you would be leaving this house. Do not act rashly and cause your mother worry," he commanded.

A few minutes later the women returned loaded with rolled maps. "Isaac, I brought the aerial maps of the entire area. I thought it might help in coordinating the search."

He kissed her cheek. "You're always a step ahead, my love."

They took seats around the desk and flattened the maps to begin planning as they waited for Marcus and Stefan.

As his remaining sons entered he stood, immediately capturing everyone's attention. "The dark haired assailant from the French Quarter was seen skulking around Rose again today and now she's missing. He wasn't seen on the property or scented but with Travis's gifts that's not surprising. Cade, I want you to command and lead the team."

"No. I'll command the team."

"Cade has always led us, Simon."

"Not anymore, Dad, I'm in charge of this operation. If you can't abide by that, I'll call my guys from the unit and use them instead."

"Simon, I forbid you as your alpha to go off half cocked on your own."

Simon charged snarling aggressively, neither he nor his wolf would submit the leadership of this rescue and he sure as hell wasn't waiting one more second. That psycho had his mate.

Isaac knocked him to the floor, pinning him in a submissive hold. "I understand your needs, son, never doubt that, but if we are going to get her back unharmed we need to do this the smart way. Use your military training and discipline. We need you to have a clear, and level head."

He held him pinned until Simon calmed, and then he offered his hand to help him up. Once Simon was standing he gathered him into a rib-cracking hug. The loving touch of his father and his alpha went a long way in calming him and his wolf.

Isaac let his breath out slowly. Simon had more right than any to lead Rose's rescue. He also had military training on his side. He held Simon's gaze. "I'm going to trust you to keep a rational head on your shoulders." Releasing his son he addressed the room, "Simon will lead the rescue team."

Cade's voice rose. "I'll call Etienne. After the encounter in the Quarter he considers Rose a valued friend. If he isn't notified he'll take it personally."

Anna pulled her phone from her pocket. "I need to call Thomas and John, Rose is their second mother and they'll insist on joining the search party. At the very least they will want to be here when you bring her home."

"Simon, what do you want each of us to do?" Isaac asked.

"Everyone make your calls, and then dress in black. Stealth is priority. If he knows we are coming he might hurt her. Mom, if there is anything you and Anna can do to hide us from Travis, I would appreciate it. Prepare for an extended search in the bayou. Travis can block your gifts so we'll be fighting as humans. That means guns and knives." He directed his gaze at Cade and Anna. "I leave in thirty. I won't delay any longer."

"That's not enough time for them to get here," Anna cried.

Simon simply looked at her, not blinking. "I'm not waiting. I leave in thirty minutes."

"She's their second mother," she protested.

He turned his head slowly, looking at her with his cold, blue eyes. "She's MY mate." His voice was flat, almost a monotone, but it carried weight and authority. He never raised his voice, but he was always heard. He spun on his heel and walked out the door.

Rose? Rose, I love you. Hang in there baby, I'm coming. Nothing. Even in sleep she should have heard him. He knew Travis could block his telepathy with his mate but he had to keep trying. Apprehension rippled through his gut. Dragging in a breath, he tamped down his growing fear. He wouldn't entertain a single thought of her injured or dead, that wasn't an option.

Rose moaned as she regained consciousness, being choked until passed out left a skull splitting headache. She didn't need to experience that again in this lifetime. Her mouth was bone dry and her throat ached. The room didn't have a mirror but she was sure there were bruises the exact shape of Travis's hands on her neck.

The door was closed allowing her secrecy to appraise her situation. Gingerly she left the bed, praying it didn't squeak or moan as her weight left it. She froze when voices rose in the next room.

"Stop mooning over the bitch and get out there for your watch."

"I'm going, but I'll be close and if you go near her I'll kill you."

"You can try, mutt."

A door slammed and more than one man laughed on the other side of her door. She remained frozen, waiting for the men to come after her but the door remained closed. There was a window in the corner and it looked large enough to fit through. *YES!* Her luck was holding, the glass pane was gone. She wouldn't even have to open it to get out. As quietly as she could she moved the chair from the corner to under the window. She stepped onto it and a loud groan came from the rickety old chair. The door slammed open and she dove for the window. Almost through, she was lifting her other leg out when a hand grabbed her ankle. Balling her hands together she slammed down on the wrist exposed. He yelped and released her. She fell to the soft ground and scrambled for the tree line.

One man came through the window after her and another came through the door. She ran for the cover of the forest. Travis appeared out of nowhere and stood between her and the other men. She rushed to the trees and let them swallow her. Not stopping she tried to put distance between herself and her kidnappers.

A fight could be heard in the distance. It sounded vicious and there was definitely more than only three guys out there.

Once undercover with a good half mile of bayou behind her, she breathed a little easier. She had to be smart about this and try to make a plan. *Okay, I have no idea where I am. Maybe if I can get near the water I'll recognize something from when we went to the bar?*

She worked her way to the water's edge and search up and down the canal. Nothing looked familiar. She slapped the billionth mosquito and eyed the water. She wasn't sure if the dark shapes were alligators or submerged logs. *Best not to find out.* The location was picturesque but desolate. Though beautiful to look at, this island offered only terror and her closest hope for help was more than likely miles away through alligator infested water. Worse yet, Simon had no more idea where to find her than she had for the direction home.

I have no food, no water, no weapons and I'm lost in the swap. I'm so screwed. Okay, I've watched all the seasons of Survivor, I can do this. A twig snapped behind her and she dove for cover. She listened hard as she remained as quiet as she could. A growl came from fifty feet to her right. She looked left and thankfully it was high dry ground with a faint game trail. She slowly moved onto the trail and away from who ever had followed her. Just when she thought she was in the clear she heard the rhythmic pounding of paws in soft earth. They were coming!

Chapter 13

On the Run

Terror was a living and breathing presence. Fear took her well past the point of thinking rationally. She had no one to rely on but herself. *I need to get the heck out of here, before they locate me.* Running now, her only thought was *stay to high ground.*

Whoever said watching TV was bad can bite me. She knew from watching national geographic and Swamp People that in the bayou an island could be deceiving. Filled with spongy sinkholes, they were everywhere. And if you find one, you can kiss your ass goodbye. An unwary traveler could fall into one, but she was safer under cover than on a path. They were stalking her and might find her again, or be waiting in ambush. She was fairly certain Travis was in the heavy undergrowth.

Snakes were a very real issue, they were everywhere and some were deadly. Thank god for eighth grade science class, she could identify all five poisonous varieties. They will all bite you but not all will kill you.

It had been hours since she escaped. She wasn't sure when she'd lost them. Or maybe they were out there right now playing cat and mouse with her, she didn't really know. He's a shifter and could trail her by scent quite easily but her instinct to survive wouldn't let her stop running even knowing it was fruitless.

Simon: Le Beau Brothers

The foul stench of stagnant water permeated the air. Disoriented, she slowed, stumbling forward until she couldn't go any farther. She fell onto the first open dry ground she found. Rose lay, waiting for them to grab her, but as the seconds ticked by, she realized they must not be ready to end his sick game yet.

Exhausted, she tried to rise. She needed to find shelter not to mention food and water. She couldn't, her body just wouldn't cooperate. It was dangerous to sleep on the open ground so she put everything she had into standing. Her only options were keep moving or find shelter.

The sun was going down and she seriously needed to find a safe place for the night. She didn't want to be in the open when the night creatures came out to play.

Nightfall was upon her and there was only a sliver of moon spilling across the swamp. In the darkness, the cypress trees looked macabre, as if they stretched long stick arms instead of branches. Grayish moss hanging like streamers looked like tattered clothes fluttering occasionally above the blackened water. The breeze barely stirred, making the muggy air barely breathable.

Stumbling forward, she broke through a line of brush to see salvation. A small cabin-style house materialized in front of her.

It looked solid enough, and in the back of her mind was the thought that if she could just make it to the door the person inside might help her.

As soon as she reached the door she new it was abandoned, *I have all the luck. At least I'll be safe from gators and snakes in there.* She pushed open the swollen door to find a one-room, bare bones hunting shack. Nothing fancy but she didn't have the luxury of pickiness.

Pushing the door until she managed to squeeze it back into its frame, she felt a little safer. She turned her efforts to searching what the little cabin may have to offer and clear it of any creepy crawlers. There were only two cabinets in the makeshift kitchen, opening the first she squealed with delight, *canned goods!* She would dine on baked beans and peaches tonight. The single drawer below produced a can opener, spoon, and a large roll of trail marking ribbon like they use on Swamp People. *YAHTZEE!*

She feasted on the beans and then relished the peaches. There was no drinking water available so she drank the juice from the can. She didn't want to dehydrate if she could help it.

The beat up single mattress sagging against the wall looked nasty so she made due with the floor. At least she was fed and had a roof over her head. The cans of beans and peaches were all the cabin had to offer and they were gone. She would have to keep moving and try to find another cabin or if she was really lucky, people. Tomorrow she would get an early start and stick close to the water. With any luck, a boat might come by.

The swamp came alive after dark. As she lay awake listening she shot off the floor. *I can speak with Simon with telepathy! Simon? Can you hear me?* She heard only silence. *He must be too far away.* She sighed. *Simon, please find me. Soon.*

She was on the verge of sleep when voices came from the forest near the cabin. Quietly she slid into a shadow along one wall.

"God dammit. Travis must have blocked her scent, she could be anywhere."

"He told us to leave her be. Claimed she was his mate now. Crazy mutt has totally lost it this time."

"We're not going to find her this way, check that cabin then we head back."

Twigs snapped below the single window and a shadow leaned toward the grimy glass. "She's not here, let's go. She'll have to come back sooner or later or starve. Unless a gator gets her."

She tried to sleep but she was terrified they would come back. Exhausted with tears rolling down her cheeks she finally dozed off.

Anna pressed the speed dial on her phone.
"Hello?"

"Hi, baby, it's Mom."

"Hey, Mom, what's up?" John asked.

"Is Thomas with you?"

"Yeah.....what's wrong, Mom? I hear it in your voice so don't deny it."

She heard him yelling for his brother to pick up the extension.

"Mom? What's wrong?" Thomas asked breathing hard. He must have run for the phone.

"Rose is missing, we think a crazed shifter has her." The stress had her chest feeling like it was squeezed in a vice and tears streamed down her face. "Awww!"

"Mom! Mom, what happened! Are you okay?"

"Yeah," she breathed through the pain. "I think I might have just had a contraction."

"Anna! What's wrong?" Cade ran into the room.

She was weeping and holding her stomach, "Cade, it's too early, he won't make it."

Cade swept her into his arms and ran to his parents' house, Anna needed his mother's healing abilities. NOW!

The phone and her sons were forgotten, as she was rushed from the house.

"I'll call Jack, you call Michael," Thomas directed John. "We're out of here in forty five minutes. If they can't be here, they'll have to follow after." He jammed what he would need into a duffle bag. "We're not waiting."

Thirty minutes later all four men were loaded into the Suburban speeding down Highway 87. Nineteen hours and they would be there, eighteen or less if they pushed it hard, and they were pushing it. They received hourly updates on their mother and the baby, she was stable and Emma had been able to stop the contractions. They needed to find Rose for both her safety and Anna's health, the stress was having detrimental effects on the pregnancy.

They drove straight through, and with the help of some old police academy buddies leading the way, it had only taken fifteen hours. Cops all along the route chaperoned the boys in their race to save Rose.

Thomas gave his brother a determined look then pulled his pistol from the glove box and exited the black Suburban. *Just in case,* he thought. He had no desire to get up close and personal with a gator. John, Michael, and Jack were gearing up as well. Their luggage would have to wait, Rose was in danger and nothing else mattered.

Glancing toward the river, male voices caught his attention as he began to arm himself. Bowie knife secured in its hip sheath, he holstered his weapon before he grabbed his rifle for good measure and struck out to join them.

The night breeze was heavy with humidity, the moonlight bright and eerie as it reflected off the black water. Simon and the men turned at the sound of boots on dock planks. A quick round of welcomes and it was back to business.

Each just over six feet in height, Thomas and the men from Denver were on the short side in this crowd. At twenty-four, most people underestimated Thomas's knowledge and experience due to his youth. Most people were wrong. He was intelligent, cunning, and deadly. He may be human but he could hold his own against even these men.

He went straight to Simon and gave him a back pounding hug. "Simon, these are Rose's foster brothers Jack and Michael," Thomas said. The men shook hands. Then Simon turned and introduced them to his brothers and father.

"Thank you for coming, I'm sure once we find her

she'll be happy to see you," Simon said to Jack and Michael. He was holding it together but just barely, it had been a day since she went missing and he was sick with worry.

Jack looked Simon in the eye. "If Rose needs us, we come, plain and simple."

He nodded his acceptance of that, glad to have these capable men in the crew.

Simon broke them into teams. "Thomas and Jack I want you with Stefan and Isaac, you'll be on point. John and Michael, you're with Cade at my flank. Etienne and Marcus, you're with me. Keep your eyes on the banks, watch for signs of her passage. I'll direct us using hand signals, speak as little as possible, silence is essential."

The boats went upstream, they had searched down stream yesterday finding no sign of Rose. They moved slowly searching for the slightest sign of her passing. When they came to a split in the channel the boats each took a branch. Eight hours later they returned to the dock without Rose.

As the boats were secured Isaac watched Simon closely. He was worried about his son's state of mind. It had been two days of searching with no sign of Rose. If it were Emma missing he'd be hysterical with worry.

He knocked on Simon's front door out of courtesy before he walked in. "Simon?"

"I'm in here," he called from the bedroom.

Isaac found Simon hugging Rose's pillow, with his nose buried in it. "How are you holding up?"

"I can't live without her, Dad." He raised his gaze. "If she isn't found, I don't want to live either."

Isaac nodded, he understood a mate's need. If he were in Simon's position he would feel the same. "Promise me you won't do anything drastic until you give us enough time to actually find her."

"I'll hold on as long as I can, but I can't hear her. I try continuously but I can't speak with her. I can't sense her, Dad. It feels like she's already gone." Tears streamed down his face as his heart shattered.

Isaac gathered his son in his arms and held him until his sobs subsided. "I can't promise we'll find her, but I can promise we'll keep searching. Just hold on a little longer, Simon." He gently wiped his son's face, kissed the top of his head and gave him some privacy.

As the team gathered at the boats the next morning, Simon announced, "I received word of a possible sighting yesterday five miles northeast of here."

The men exchanged glances but remained silent.

"I have reason to believe she wasn't kidnapped but is being chased or hunted."

Gasps raced through the boats. "What makes you suspect that?" Stefan asked.

"I was told she was seen running and looking behind herself, they said she looked terrified and thought they glimpsed a wolf stalking her. Before they could help her, she disappeared and they were unable to relocate her. They also said that while searching, a trail marked by ribbon on trees was found. They followed it to an abandoned cabin. I believe the trail was marked by Rose."

"We'll have to search in a completely different fashion than we normally would, instead of searching for a specific scent you are searching for a complete lack of scent." He looked to Thomas. "You have the right idea, we'll need to use brute force, guns, and knives initially to subdue him and shut down his gift. Our powers won't work against him until he is unconscious or dead."

Chapter 14

Rescue

Sweat beaded her brow in the Louisiana early morning sun. Without taking her gaze from the surrounding swamp, she wiped away the perspiration. Every second counted, and she had to stay ready. Rose scanned her surroundings, she needed to hide and catch her breath. Crouched in a thicket, she held her position, watching, listening. All she heard were birds chirping, the light patter of raindrops on the leaves, and a distant roll of thunder. A reassuring thought crossed her mind, she could gage if danger was close to her through insect and bird reactions. *I must be safe for the moment or the birds would be silent. And, they haven't been spooked away, that's a good sign too.*

She was on the move again. She tiptoed across a spongy patch of ground as fast as she could while avoiding noisy twigs and debris. Out of the corner of her eye, something large and solid caught her attention. *Could I really be this lucky?* An abandoned cabin appeared as she parted the tall grass she had been using as cover. It looked like it had been more than a hunting shack in is heyday.

Using any cover available and staying to the shadows she made her way to the door and slipped through. Cobwebs covered the cabinets and dust layered every surface. Quietly, she closed the door and barred it as best she could.

My kingdom for a meal and a bed she thought as she leaned against the door, hardly able to stand. She was pretty sure it had been three days since she had been drawn into the woods and kidnapped by Travis. Two of those days without food and with little sleep to speak of.

Why was Travis protecting her from the others? Was he really crazy enough to think he could force her to be his mate? From what she knew it didn't work that way. She was trying in vain to find her way back to Simon. Hanging her head, she admitted to herself she was hopelessly lost. Unlike the hunting shack, there wasn't a stitch of food in this cabin but it did provide shelter. She decided to explore more and if she didn't find help or another cabin by the time it got dark she would follow her ribbons back to this one.

Simon directed the team to avoid the pier and instead docked the boats at a hidden strip of trail that led to the center of the island.

"Stefan, direct the alligators and snakes into the river and away from us. I don't want anyone bit."

"Got it, bro."

They eased the boats into a small inlet one hundred feet from the dock and around a bend, out of sight. The men slipped into the knee-deep water, pulling the boats behind them to tie to a tree or shrub. It was a painstakingly slow process, taking care not to splash as they struggled through the mire until they could reach higher ground. Like all bogs, grass grew wild and tall and a multitude of shrubbery and flowers filled in spaces between trees.

The team moved in silence. Simon directed them to avoid dry twigs and leaves, and with Stefan's animal communication abilities, they were able to keep the remaining wildlife from giving away their presence.

"He's here," Simon said as he eyed fresh paw prints on the muddy riverbank with malice.

"How do you know it's him?" Cade asked.

Simon rested his rifle on his shoulder. "I know his print. When he came to the plantation I made a point of inspecting both sets of tracks." He growled as he imagined Rose's fear. Scanning the area, he zeroed in on a fluttering ribbon. "Rose is close." He smiled and breathed her name like a prayer.

"Did you find something?" Isaac asked as he joined him.

"Her mark is on that tree." He pointed.

He ordered the men to fan out and search for more ribbons and tracks. Using his empathy, he closed his eyes...nothing. He knew it was a long shot but he had to keep trying. He looked left and right and saw no sign of the men. That gave him his second small smile since Rose's disappearance, his team was the best there was.

After returning to the empty cabin for shelter she had managed to sleep for a few hours. With an unsatisfied stomach and no other option, she once again left the cabin to wonder through the swamp praying that today she would find her way home.

She stepped carefully along the trail, through hard won experience, she knew what the edges of a sinkhole looked like. An alligator growled somewhere nearby followed by a splash. She glanced in the direction of the sound, quickly verifying the creature's location.

Travis waited, out there somewhere and her only option was to keep moving until she found civilization. She had made her way through miles of swamp and bog. A miracle by any standard if she dared look at it closely.

Much more had gone right than wrong, she had found food and shelter and wasn't dead. She kept telling herself that Simon would be waiting for her. She knew he was telepathic, so why wasn't he answering her? For the hundredth time she wondered if the telepathy thing had a distance limit.

Rose paused, her body swaying with exhaustion. She went still, a shadow moved in the darkness to her left. She took three steps to her right, ducking into a shadow.

She had learned patience over the last few days. She pushed her weariness aside and waited. Listened. Watched. There was only the occasional plop of a snake dropping from overhead branches into the murky waters. Still, she waited, knowing movement drew the eye.

Stay quiet and don't move, Rose chanted to herself. Her muscles quivered and burned from maintaining her position.

It didn't matter how many deep breaths she took, she was in serious trouble and would be discovered any second. She heard more than one person or animal. She wasn't sure if they were moving close to her. Her only option was to remain hidden until she could verify what moved in the shadows. It could be a threat as easily as a rescue party.

Simon wanted to disembowel the wolf that had taken his mate but they needed to verify Rose was safe first. He may need to be questioned. Never fear, you bastard, death will shake your hand soon enough. Silently he commanded his team with hand signals. Each wolf or man moved into striking distance with impressive precision. Simon crept forward into position; from there he heard and saw everything that went down.

Birds screeched and rose like a cloud into the air. Simon looked toward the sound. He shifted his position and peered through a thick hedge of saw grass. He heard the distinct crackle of a radio and instantly dropped to the ground. He remained motionless, barely breathing, until he could determine the exact position of Travis.

Sound carried on the water making the conversation easy to hear. Simon stiffened, that was one of the men Rose had described for him. One of her muggers. She had called them Dark Hair, Blondie, and Scruffy. Dark Hair's gaze kept straying toward the old cabin. Rose was in there.

His ears immediately tuned to Dark Hair's conversation over a static-filled radio.

"So, did you do it?"

Simon cocked his head at the anxious, unfamiliar male voice. Ah, the beauty of his shifter powers. He had hearing that would make a bat jealous. And he knew the topic of their discussion…

Rose.

"She'll never find her way back. I expect the final payment in the account immediately," Dark Hair radioed back.

"You'll get paid once her death is verified and not before. It'll do no good to have her miraculously survive."

"That wasn't our deal, we drove her into the heart of the bayou. That was our agreement. We want our money or we'll continue to let her run and she might find her way back to the Le Beaus'."

"If you want it now, you have to kill her, otherwise you'll wait." The static abruptly went silent marking the end to the conversation.

The muscle in Simon's jaw started to tic in time to his rapid, angry heartbeat as he listened. It took incredible stealth for Simon to get within striking distance of his prey. He watched Dark Hair rake his fingers through his hair, undoubtedly deciding his next move.

Time to put Operation Rose into high gear.

He held his position, satisfied for the moment that Rose was not his captive, and waited for his team to signal 'all clear.' Instead of the birdcalls he heard frog croaks and gator growls. It wasn't clear. They were in for a fight.

He gave the signal to ready themselves for battle then waited to the count of twenty for each man to get into his best striking position.

Simon rose from the grass hedge like a giant shadow, inches from taking Dark Hair down. At the last heartbeat the man spun to attack.

Simon swept Dark Hair's legs from under him then struck with his Bowie. Dark Hair dodged the strike and nailed Simon with a right hook.

With a roar, Simon grabbed Dark Hair's right arm and snapped it above the elbow. The man screamed in pain. Before Simon could subdue him or finish him off Dark Hair pulled a knife and slashed wildly. Simon eluded the sharp blade watching for his opening.

Behind him Stefan, Thomas, and Jack fought Blondie. Thomas was thrown ten feet and crashed into a tree. Jack crouched, Bowie in hand, as Stefan circled waiting for his chance to strike.

As Blondie lunged at Jack, Rose's brother made a rapid up-slash and across the man's mid section before Blondie could disarm him. At the same moment, Thomas fired his rifle, blowing out Blondie's knee. Blondie screamed and staggered back into Stefan's waiting hands. One quick twist of his neck and the scream stopped.

To Simon's left, Cade fought a fourth man with John and Michael. The man swiped at John with a knife but the boy was fast, really fast, and he avoided the blade. Using a spin kick John struck the man in the jaw with a shattering force. The man faltered then regained his balance. Before the man could recover all his wits, Michael struck with his Bowie driving it deep into his belly. As the man doubled over Cade gave his neck a quick twist in the same manner Stefan had.

Simon tired of the knife play with Dark Hair, he flipped his knife so the blade landed in perfect throwing position and let it fly. The Bowie rested in Dark Hair's heart up to the hilt. Gurgling and drooling blood, Dark Hair crumpled to the ground.

Simon had a reputation before entering the Marines as a man who didn't lose in a fight, now he was downright lethal. His deadly gaze zeroed in on Travis, held by Etienne and Isaac. Marcus was searching the area for additional men.

Simon roughly snatched Travis from Etienne. "I want nothing more than to snap your neck at this very moment but that will have to wait," he hissed into his ear then shoved him back into Etienne's waiting hands.

He couldn't kill him until he had Rose in his arms, he might need to interrogate him. "Father, Et, hold him while I check for Rose." He raced across the clearing, he couldn't reach her fast enough. As he neared the cabins door he heard nothing, it was silent. "Rose? Rose are you here?" A quick scan of the one room shack proved it was empty.

A red haze of fury, spread across his vision. He charged Travis, grabbed a handful of hair and yanked his head back. "Where the hell is she, Travis!"

He glared at Simon then spit in his face.

Simon seized Travis from Etienne's grasp and smashed his fist into his jaw, a crack rang out as the bone shattered. Rapid blows to his ribs, pulverized half of his rib cage. Until the force of his fists was the only thing keeping Travis on his feet. Simon shoved him toward Cade and watched him fall to his knees.

Bending to snarl in his ear. "I said, where is she?" The menace in his demand spoke of a long painful death.

"Go to hell, Le Beau," he wheezed. Blood poured

down Travis's face and soaked his torn shirt. He spit a mouthful on the ground along with two teeth. Throwing back his head, he laughed a hair raising maniacal cackle. "She's long gone, and you're never going to find her."

With a roar, Simon slashed his knife across the man's exposed chest. Blood gushed from the deep cut.

Travis screamed and attempted to shift, nothing happened. "What the fuck!"

"You can't shift unless I will it," Isaac said calmly.

"What does that mean," he growled.

Shrugging, Isaac's lip curled on one end. "I'm king. I control your ability to shift or not as I see fit."

Enraged by Isaac's decree, Travis broke free and lunged at Michael and Jack. A knife flashed.

Michael blocked the initial attack with his arm. A stream of blood painted the forest crimson. Jack put Travis in a chokehold but the blood covering him made his grip slip.

Stefan grabbed Travis but before he could subdue him, Travis spun right and slashed Michael across his mid section then left across Jack's throat.

Michael screamed in agony and watched in horror as his large intestine spilled into his hands. His face drained to deathly pale and he slid to the ground as he lost consciousness.

With an insane gleam in his eyes Travis turned on Thomas but he was ready and planted a slug to his chest. When he kept coming, he flipped him to the ground.

Travis snarled and got to his knees as he attempted to stand again.

Hearing the commotion, Rose moved from where she was hiding. She reached the edge of the tree line as Travis slashed Jack and all hell broke loose.

Rose's eyes narrowed at the sight of Travis harming her brothers. A buzz began in her mind as an unbridled fury boiled deep in her gut. She'd never felt such rage. It rose like a tsunami. She wanted blood. Travis's blood.

A large rock lay at her feet, much heavier than she should be able to lift. She scooped it up and bellowed her fury as she launched herself from her hiding place.

Travis turned on her, ready to fight.

For a fleeting instant, fear gripped her, one glance at her brothers and it was gone, washed away by her roiling rage. Raising the rock high she smashed him in the head with it as he was drawing back his knife. His bloody body crumpled to the ground, out cold. Panting from the adrenalin racing in her blood she put her hands on her knees to catch her breath. She didn't drop her rock though. She eyed Travis, not trusting he was really out.

A collective gasp told her the men had all witness her avenging her brothers.

Large arms came from behind to wrap around her, she reacted on instinct raising her rock to strike. Isaac stopped her at the last second from bashing Simon. "Rose, dear, please don't beat your mate."

It took a heartbeat to realize Simon was really

there. She threw her arms around his neck, weeping from relief or loss she wasn't sure.

Simon couldn't hold her close enough. She raised her head and his blue gaze collided with her tormented one. Air rushed into his body and for the first time in days he took her scent with it. He should have smelled the swamp, but instead he smelled woman. *Rose*.

Turning in his arms, Rose's heart ripped from her chest as the life she'd known since she was twelve collapsed. Michael was bleeding out and Jack clutched his slashed throat. These were her brothers, the only family she'd had. They had created a bubble of safety around her and provided the first place she'd ever felt truly safe and secure. Not a family exactly, but certainly as close as a foster child could come. Now her family was dying before her eyes. Because of her.

Etienne locked gazes with her, his face grim. "I should've been able to prevent this." He swore. "I am so sorry, mon ami." He turned to Simon. "What would you have of me?"

"Can you help them? Please, Simon, do something," Rose cried.

Simon held her, giving as much comfort as he could. "Etienne, is there anything you can do?"

Etienne felt for a pulse, Michael was white as a sheet and barely breathing. "They are still alive, but barely." Etienne gazed at Rose with sadness in his eyes.

Rose pinned Etienne with her pleading eyes. "Please."

Etienne stepped forward and gave her one regal nod. "I can turn them but they must choose it."

Cade and Marcus were already attending the

wounded humans, doing what they could.

She tore from Simon's arms and threw herself on the ground next to Jack and Michael. "Don't die, oh please, don't die," she cried. She was so distressed after witnessing their attack she was on the verge of hyperventilating. "Can you hear me? Do you want Etienne to make you a vampire? If you do, nod once."

Both men gave a weak nod.

"Etienne! Hurry! What are you waiting for? Damn it move!"

"Come on, cher, give Etienne room." Simon gripped her shoulders helping her to stand.

"Not until he saves them." A bulldozer wasn't going to move her right now. She would stand, but she wasn't leaving just yet.

Etienne began giving instructions to Cade and Marcus, time was of the essence if he was going to save both men.

"Rose," Simon's voice sounded like a prayer. He took Rose's face in his hands and kissed her like his life depended on it. He had his heart and soul back in his arms. He ran his hands over her, as if convincing himself she was in one piece.

She clung to him, washed in relief at his presence and yet refusing to take her eyes from the gruesome scene before her.

His chest rumbled as he kissed her forehead. "I've been searching the bayou for you."

"I tried to find my way back, but I was knocked out when I was brought out here and had no idea which way to go."

He took possession of her lips again, it would be a

long time before he would be able to release her from his hold. The world had dropped away for them and time stopped. He had his reason for living again.

Etienne spoke softly. "I have completed the exchange, they will rest for a few days and then rise as vampires. They will need time to adjust so you won't see them for a while."

Rose let out a long breath. She almost collapsed in relief but Simon held her too tightly to fall. "Thank you, Etienne, I can't thank you enough for what you have done for them."

"My pleasure, mon ami, it will be a very different existence for them. I don't want you to be upset when you see them and they are your brothers but different."

"I'll take them any way I can get them," she insisted.

"Simon, may I?" He took her from Simon's arms and hugged her tightly for a moment. "I am sorry I didn't protect them."

"You did everything you could, please don't blame yourself. Travis is the only one to blame."

He gave a single small nod, released her back to Simon, and moved away from the crowd toward the waiting boats.

"Well, now," Stefan drawled with a wicked glint in his eyes as he gave her an appreciative look, "all I can say is I'm never going to piss you off." He looked pointedly at the stone she still clutched.

She smiled weakly at that and tossed her rock in the air, catching it again. "Just don't chase me for days through the bayou and we'll get along just fine."

Stefan's grin widened. "I like her, Simon, I think

you should keep her."

Isaac cleared his throat. Taking her shoulders, he looked into her eyes. "Rose, are you hurt at all? Hungry perhaps?"

Rose was about to answer, but she saw Travis move out of the corner of her eye. Before the men could react, she smashed him in the head again.

Travis collapsed to the ground and Marcus rushed forward to secure him before he had the chance to attempt anything else.

Rose stood over him glaring. "I really hate you, Travis, I've only hated one person in my life but I can honestly say I hate you too. Do yourself a favor and don't move again. If you do, I'll use a bigger rock."

Stefan chuckled. He liked a woman with gumption. And awesome skills with a rock. "You're one lucky bastard, brother," he slapped Simon on the back then joined the others at the boats.

Simon's face was a mixture of amusement and absolute relief. He glanced at the cabin. "It isn't a five-star hotel, is it?"

"Definitely not the Ritz," she agreed. She was trying to see what was happening with her brothers but Simon stepped into her line of sight.

"Mon amour, you don't need to watch that. I have food and water in the boat. Come on, let me take care of my mate. I don't plan to let you out of my sight for the next ten years and then I'll think about it."

Cade stepped away from the group surrounding Jack and Michael. "They're going to be fine. When you are feeling up to it, I'll explain what to expect from them as vampires."

She searched his face, and with one last glance in her brothers' direction she nodded.

Simon wrapped her in his arms again and she allowed him to lead her to the boat.

"I want to go home," Rose pleaded quietly to Simon. "Please, take me home."

"Do you mean Denver?" His expression was drawn and leery.

She shook her head. "No, 'our' home."

Three days later, Simon helped Rose into his boat. They'd been asked to attend the verdict of Travis's trial at his pack's plantation.

Travis's long matted brown hair was straggly and fell down his back in unkempt, untidy clumps. Arms wrapped around his knees, he rocked himself on the floor, moaning softly. His eyes popped open and darted to the two-way mirror, as black as midnight and as penetrating as steel.

Rose winced visibly and turned into Simon's chest, when the disturbed creature turned those tortured eyes in her direction.

"He can't see you through the glass," he whispered in reassurance. Simon swept his arm around Rose and bent his head to hers. "You have tears in your eyes."

"I know, I feel justified with his sentence," Rose said and blinked rapidly. "But, I can't help but feel terrible for his uncle. How is he going to live with taking his nephew's life? Are there any options other than death, or can't someone else do it?" Rose whispered.

"Nothing we've tried has worked, and Travis is my responsibility," Jason answered solemnly as he joined them.

A maniacal cackle sounded through the two-way mirror. "They'll never stop. All of your women will die terrible bloody deaths. A new reign approaches, ready to take the throne from the absent king." Travis stopped speaking as abruptly as he began.

Isaac studied the madness in Travis's eyes before meeting the elder's gaze with heartbreaking resolve. Grasping the man's forearms in a long forgotten sign of respect from one warrior to another, he took a moment before he spoke. "My son tasked you with this responsibility, his crime is unforgivable and law demands the end of his existence. Ordering one family member to end another brings me nothing but pain. I'm sorry, I have no choice but to require you to carry out this heinous sentence." He indicated for Jason to enter Travis's room.

Jason, took a deep breath and pushed open the door to the small cell.

Isaac sighed. "Clear the room, and give them a moment of privacy. The least we could do is allow them a final goodbye."

Jason held Travis in his arms. After a minute he pulled Travis to his feet and along with the assigned witnesses led him from the building and into the nearby forest.

The Le Beaus and all of the elders from the local packs gathered on the lawn. The birds and wildlife went silent seconds before a mournful howl rang out. The witnesses emerged from the forest and gave a single nod to Isaac.

Before leaving, the elders approached Isaac. "We'd like to have an official meeting with you to discuss the issues that have been occurring within the packs. Are you willing to meet with us, my lord?" the spokesman of the group asked.

Isaac looked over the expectant faces eagerly awaiting his response. "Yes, I think it's time. I'll have Emma contact each of you with a date and time."

Chapter 15

The Claiming

Travis hadn't given them the names of the men behind Rose's kidnapping. All Simon knew was someone wanted to take the seat of power and reign as the new king. Neither the Le Beaus nor the elders from the packs wanted that to happen.

If the other shifters, whoever they were, wanted to challenge the Le Beaus, bring it. At least now they were forewarned. And as his assault team proved, fore-armed. If they wanted to take them on, then Simon wished them luck. They were going to need it and a whole lot of reinforcements.

He surprisingly was looking forward to the challenge. He hadn't felt this normal since before his enlistment. *I'm back!*

Simon held open the front door to their house for Rose, he wouldn't be happy until he had her safely in their home. The threat from Travis was gone but there were others at play in this deadly game.

"Someone is out to get you and Anna. There's a war brewing over who'll lead the shifter community. We need to find out who before the situation gets worse. If they're willing to kidnap you and drive you into the belly of the bayou, they're capable of anything."

"Are you sure? Is Anna in danger, too? Oh my god, is Cade protecting her?"

"She is well guarded, you can be assured of that so don't worry."

"You do know I can take care of myself, right? I may be a soft city girl but I survived days out there on my own. Not that I don't appreciate the rescue, mind you." She ran her finger down his chest.

"Baby, after seeing you in action with nothing but a rock, I have nothing but respect for your ability to take care of things. But, I hope you'll humor me and pretend that you let me keep you safe." He grinned boyishly. "My ego and my wolf have taken enough of a beating over this already."

"I think I can play the damsel in distress once in a while." She stood on tiptoes and kissed his cheek.

With his heart in his eyes, he leaned down and kissed her soft lips. "Thank you." The touch of her lips re-ignited the heat that was always so close to the surface. "You're always surprising me. I like it."

Collecting every ounce of courage she had, she slipped her hand into his and gently tugged him toward the loveseat in the living room. Simon wrapped his arms around her and she snuggled as close as she could get. He stroked her hair and rubbed his chin across the top of her head. A few minutes passed before Rose spoke.

"I said I wanted to complete the ritual. Now that my stalker is no longer a threat we need to talk." She pulled away to face him.

"You sound very serious, do I need to be concerned?" His lips drew into a frown.

"I had a lot of time to think over the past few days. I want to provide a full disclosure of who I am. You need to know a few things about me." She took a deep breath. "When I was young, foster kids weren't always treated very well. All of the homes I was in were wonderful, except one. That's where I met Jack and Michael."

"Rose…"

Raising her hand, "Please, let me finish. We had to steal food and clothing to survive and I got caught. Our foster father had a taste for young girls." She looked to the floor afraid to see his reaction.

A ferocious snarl caused her eyes to jump to his. "Give me his name," he demanded.

Her mind recalled that life-shattering day, taking her back in time.

She was too terrified to cry.

At the slam of the front door, she pressed herself further into the back of the closet. Her twelve-year-old body shrank behind a beat up cardboard box, its sides and flaps worn and breaking apart. Her heart hammered as she held herself to stop the trembling. Quiet. She must be quiet. He couldn't be allowed to hear her.

Tightly she closed her eyes and let her mind drift to another place, the safe place she visited when things got too bad. Her body lay on the soft cool grass in her dreams. She was protected, safe.

For a fleeting moment, the terror went away.

Please, don't let him find me.

Her prayer went unanswered. Heavy footsteps crossed the scuffed and gouged wooden floor toward her hiding place. With a grunt he jerked open the closet and yanked her out. He drew back his fist…this was going to be bad.

Shaking her head, Rose dispelled the nightmare. "He died years ago. He's no longer a threat to anyone. He managed to get me alone once, please don't ask me to go into detail…yes, he did what you're thinking and I survived. After that Jack and Michael made sure at least one of them was with me at all times. They even took turns sleeping on the floor next to my bed. He never got near me again and shortly thereafter we were all moved to another home."

He was clenching his fist so tightly his knuckles were white.

She gave him time to absorb all she had said. "Now you know the truth," she said. "I've stolen things. I've been arrested for shoplifting. A foster parent abused me. And I have no solid basis for having a healthy family or raising children. Are you sure you want to claim someone so broken as your mate?"

He couldn't begin to tell her how wrong she was about herself. He simply stared at her, stunned into silence.

"That's what I thought."

Rose raced for the door. She swiped at her eyes with the back of her hand and fumbled trying to unlock the screen door, giving Simon enough time to reach her and whirl her in his arms, pinning her against the door. Her face, streaked with tears, tore at his soul. He had to make her listen.

"Aren't you going to give me the chance to respond? You just took out a crazy stalker with a rock! I can't believe a strong woman like you would run like a coward."

She paused, open-mouthed. "I...don't understand."

"Do you want to know what I see when I look at you? I don't see a thief or the victim of a horrid childhood. You've already overcome more hardships than most people will ever face in a lifetime. The child you were, shaped the woman you are, and she's amazing and beautiful and...everything I ever dreamed of."

Her chin quivered and she shuddered with a flood of emotions.

"Rose, I know that you're afraid of having your heart shattered. I promise you, I'll never leave you, never reject you or deny you. You would be my choice even without the mating attraction." He wiped a tear from her cheek.

He repositioned, sliding his leg between hers so she could feel the power she had over him. She molded against him, pressing into his length. His entire body hardened further with a desire he could barely control. He'd been waiting for this since the moment he'd gotten her back.

"I want you, Rose, as my mate. Badly." He lowered his head, nipped lightly at her ear and nuzzled her neck, smiling as her pulse jumped beneath his lips. He kissed the top of her head as he stroked her arms and he linked his fingers with hers. When she kept her face buried in his chest, he pulled back to study her. With a gentle hand, he tilted her chin up and stared into the caution on her face. He lifted her hand to his lips and turned her palm over to kiss the center, relishing her racing pulse, knowing he was the cause. "I want you, Rose, only you."

Rose gulped in a tear-choked breath. "I didn't think…"

"What? That I wouldn't want you?" He worked his way up to her neck, and breathed in deeply. "That I wouldn't want to inhale your scent?" His entire body ached with longing. He met her gaze, trembling with desire. "That I wouldn't want to make love to you? I need you more than air. More than life itself."

She wrapped her arms around his neck; her hold bordered on desperate. Running her hands down his arms, his chest, circling his waist, and finally to his hips. "I want you, too," she said with confidence finally ringing in her voice. "I think it's the stress from thinking I'd never see you again. I imagined all kinds of horrible things while I was lost. I'm sorry, I'm being stupid."

"No, cher, you just survived a terrifying experience and it caused you to doubt yourself and me. You believe me, right?"

She nodded and sniffed. "Take me to bed?" A blush colored her beautiful face. The woman really was making a habit of stealing his breath.

"Your wish is my command," he growled.

She fastened her lips to his, her mouth begging for entrance. He let her have her way with him. Gloried in the taste of her. With a low groan, Simon scooped her into his arms, cradling her against his chest. He almost stumbled when her lips exploring his neck, instinctively found the spot she would mark him. Shoving aside any concerns about safety issues, he held her fast and kicked open the bedroom door.

She wanted to shout for joy. Simon still wanted her, even after she put her life under a microscope for him to see. She wanted him terribly, needed him to finally create the family she had always desired, yet never had. Still, she'd been prepared for him to turn from her in disgust. He hadn't. He was here. With her. He *wanted* her. *I'll never doubt his love again.*

A weight lifted, freeing the desire she'd tamped down with her unfounded doubt. She craved his love, his touch, his caress. Her body screamed for the sensation of his lips and hands exploring her, making her body hum with sensations only he could arouse. With a thrill of anticipation, she kissed and nibbled his neck as he carried her to the bed.

A low growl rumbled in his chest. He gently laid her on their sheets. She sank into the soft mattress stretching languidly. Unwilling to relinquish his touch, she drew him down with her.

He followed willingly. His finger trailed the side of her neck, his thumb brushing the hollow in her throat, tracing her collarbone. The intensity in his eyes made her shiver. He didn't look away. He held her gaze as if he could see into her soul.

Everything she'd ever wanted sizzled in his gaze. She saw no doubt, no judgments, just hot, raw desire.

Her body quivered with eagerness. He didn't move. He simply drank her in.

"What are you doing?" Rose didn't recognize her voice, husky, longing, needy.

"I'm memorizing you," he said searching her face. "The golden flecks in your blue eyes, burning for me.

The flush of your cheeks. Your lips swollen from my kisses."

Her body was on fire, *I want to do the ritual with you. Right now.* She held his gaze and purposely spoke to him telepathically. Her hand crept down his shirtfront, slipping the buttons free one by one. She laid her palm flat and slipped past his waist and lightly over the bulge in his jeans, stopping to cup him gently.

Ever so slowly, he lowered his lips to hers. "Are you sure you are ready for the ritual?" he whispered, as his mouth hovered. "I'll wait for you, as long as it takes."

"Absolutely."

His chest rumbled and he held her face in his hands. "I'm yours, Rose. Always." He ran his fingers from her neck to her heated core then he slowly rose from the bed. Simon let his gapping shirt slide from his shoulders to pool on the floor. With his passion glowing in his eyes he popped the button of his jeans. The whisk of his zipper broke the silence of the room. Her breath sucked in as he eased his jeans down his hips.

He kicked them aside and wrapped his fist around his painful erection. He watched her eyes darken with arousal. Her eyes were intent on following the stroke of his hand.

Simon was pure temptation, standing with his wicked smile and his dark, mesmerizing eyes. Her tongue darted out and moistened her lower lip. His body took on a life of its own, nearly jumping out of his hand. "Rose," he groaned, "I need you."

Extending his hand he helped her from the bed. "I think it's time to do something new. After thinking I'd lost you forever, my wolf and I are very dominant right now. Are you able to give me control? I don't want you to be frightened or apprehensive at any moment."

She nibbled her fingernail. "That sounds exciting." Her brows furrowed. "You're not into BDSM or anything are you? I don't do pain."

He gave her a sexy lopsided grin as his eyes scorched her from head to toe.

"No, my love. Unbutton your shirt. I want to look at you." His voice was so husky, so raw with hunger, it sent a shiver down her spine.

Rose slipped the buttons free and let her blouse fall. A ray of sun peaking through the blinds caressed her breasts. Providing a spectacular spotlight. Boldly, she cupped the weight of them in her hands. She was achy, tight, and swollen. But her hungry gaze remained on his enormous erection and the drop of moisture glistening in anticipation of their mating. She took another step toward him, biting her lower lip, liking what she saw.

"Take off your jeans," he growled huskily, maintaining his even steady strokes.

She shivered in anticipation and did as he ordered. She pushed her jeans and panties from her hips and down her legs, stepping out of them. She stood before him bare as the moment she was born. She watched his chest rising and falling as his breath quicken. Saw his hand tighten, glide smoothly up and down once, twice, in an effort to get relief.

Thrilled with her newfound confidence, her hand

covered his, the other slid lower to cup and squeeze his sac gently. Her palms slid over his hips and thighs as she knelt in front of him. Even though she was unsure of how to do this, the draw of his erection trumped her doubts. She wanted him with a fierce intensity she'd been too guarded to show.

Simon's breath slammed out of his lungs, leaving him gasping for air. Her mouth slid over him, hot and moist and as tight as a fist. Her tongue danced along his ultrasensitive rim, sending jolts down his spine and his hips jerking. She'd taken his fantasy right out of his head, all his thoughts as he'd piloted the boat home that morning, and now she was putting them into action.

Her mouth was a miracle of heat. He dug his fingers deep in her hair, urging her on while his hips began to follow the rhythm she set. He fought to allow her to lead for the moment.

His eyes rolled in his head when she ran her tongue around the tip. Simon's teeth clenched and every muscle tightened. His blood sang and heart pounded.

She performed an amazing dance with her tongue and then suckled as if he were her favorite flavor of lollypop.

He sensed the combination of her need and love, felt it as his own. Very little of his brain functioned. At this point in time, he wasn't sure he knew his own name. He could only feel—and comply. She tantalized and tormented until he was certain he would detonate.

His wolf growled deep in his throat. He didn't want her to stop but he needed to hold off for the ritual. He gently tugged her hair, a small pull, exerting pressure. Even the sleek strands in his fists felt perfect. She licked her lips, as he helped her to her feet.

His hands slid over her body. Kneading her breasts, he bent his head to claim her full lips. He needed to nibble that lower lip, the hunger for her nearly driving him insane. He parted her thighs with his knee so his hand could glide down her stomach to her shaved mound. She was moist with desire, drenched for him. Ready for him.

He craved her hot, slick sweetness.

As his finger pushed into her channel, she cried "Simon," her breath coming in gasps.

He stroked deeper, encouraging her to ride his fingers, wanting her to be in the same frenzy he was.

Only when she was gasping, her body rocking and clenching, wave after wave, did he slow his fingers. He eyed the bed, he'd planned to lay her down but changed his mind. He wanted to show her the pleasures of allowing him to be in control.

He turned her toward the bed and applied enough pressure to her shoulders to bend her over so the curve of her bottom was thrust upward for him. His mouth was as dry as the desert and he gulped a breath. "You are exquisite."

He admired his beautiful, incredible mate, then ran his palms from her back to the luscious globes of her bottom. He parted her cheeks and rubbed his erection along the silken seam of her exquisite ass. He licked his lips, she was perfection, no hard boney ass on her. His teeth itched to nip her left cheek, he bent and gave it a lick and scraped his teeth lightly. She was hot and slick, quivering in anticipation, she moved to straighten and received a playful slap on her butt for her effort. He rubbed the spot and bent to her ear.

"I like the view. I'm going to pleasure you until you scream my name."

She groaned and pushed back, trying to get relief, but he held her in place, prolonging the moment, enjoying the contact and the sight of her glistening folds. His wolf tried to push forward, a feral lust building his wild need to claim her.

He slid in slowly, teasing her to build her need. Her sheath swallowed every inch of him greedily, so tight he gritted his teeth to delay his release. He was buried to the hilt, rocking his hips he thrust harder, driving into her over and over with long, maddeningly slow strokes. She bucked trying to find the release he was denying her. She whimpered as her muscles clenched and grasped at him.

Nothing mattered but her velvet friction on his straining length, so tight he knew he chanced cuming too soon. He risked it, pulling her back toward him with each stroke, riding her hard and furiously. He needed to join her body to his forever. He pounded into her, and she pushed back just as frantically, crying out her pleasure, completely uninhibited with him.

He gripped her hips to still her movement.

Licking his finger for lubrication, he slowly ran his palm around her hip. He worshipped her soft skin as he slid his finger between her thighs, circling her clit while refusing to let her move.

"Are you ready, Rose? This is your last chance to change your mind."

"Yes," she panted. "Move, damn it!"

He began shallow thrusts. "Will you give yourself body and soul to complete this man and his wolf? Will you unite your life with mine, bond your future with mine, and merge your half of our soul to mine and in doing so complete the mating ritual?" He held her still with one hand and moistened his thumb to tease her pink puckered anus. "Have you ever been pleasured here?" he whispered next to her ear.

She gasped at his touch and shook her head, no man had ever touched her there.

"I will give myself body and soul to complete you as a man and his wolf. I will unite my life with yours, bond my future to yours, and merge my half of our soul with yours. I will complete the mating ritual with you."

He laid hot little kisses down her spine as his fingers drove her wild.

She gave a little squeak when his thumb eased in one joint. He made love to her slowly as he shallowly penetrated her from behind. The arousal Simon fueled was about to push her over the edge.

He took his time, her little mewling sounds driving him crazy. Then he pushed his thumb a little deeper, filling her more fully and increasing their pleasure. She desperately tried to buck against him.

He drove her higher and higher, stroking in and out. Before she orgasmed, he removed his thumb, and, thrust powerfully. "I claim you as my mate." The magic swirled around them with his first words. "I belong to you as you belong to me. I give you my heart and my body. I will protect you even with my life. I give you all I am. I share my half of our soul to complete you. I share my magic with you." Simon rocked forward and nuzzled her neck, lapping at the spot where he would bite her. He bit quickly, piercing the flesh.

Rose cried out as the shock of pain faded to pure bliss.

He licked gently soothing the bite as he started his thrusting again.

"I beseech the great Luna Goddess to bless you and your wolf guardian. You are my mate to cherish today and for all time. I claim you as my mate."

She felt her wolf soul enter her body, it made her feel fuller, and for the first time, complete. She knew she wouldn't feel odd or out of place anymore.

He pulled from her and laid on the bed, pulling her on top. "Now you need to repeat the words back to me, my love, and bite me right here." He tapped his neck.

Standing him upright she eased onto him and began a delicious ride. It was her turn to drive him wild. When his eyes took on a crazed expression and his growling became fierce she began to speak. "I claim you as my mate. I belong to you as you belong to me. I give you my heart and my body. I will protect you even with my life. I give you all I am. I share my half of our soul to complete you."

Their souls knitting together gave her a charge of energy. The completeness made her throw her head back and laugh. She leaned forward and took his face in her hands. He was kissed like he had never been kissed before. With one final suck on his lower lip she locked her gaze to his. "I share my magic with you." She hovered over his neck blowing warm air across his skin. His shiver and goose bumped flesh distracted her and fueled her need. Razor sharp canines erupted in her mouth, jolting her into focus. She suckled his neck gave him a nip and bit down piercing his flesh.

Simon moaned as her teeth sank deep, he felt the same erotic experience she had. Gripping her hips, he flipped her under him. Straining to hold off his release. "Rose you need to finish it NOW!"

Speaking as fast as she could, "I beseech the great Luna Goddess to bless you and your wolf guardian. You are my mate to cherish today and for all time. I claim you as my mate."

With the ritual words completed, he erupted into her with a roar that rattled the windowpane. As soon as his eyesight cleared he started thrusting again, building her arousal to a fever pitch. Reaching between them he stroked her, sending her over the edge. Then he collapsed next to her.

She would never get enough of this man and the pleasure he could wring from her body.

I can't believe you're mine, really mine.

"Holy shit," she breathed, reaching up to run her fingers through his mussed hair.

"I agree one hundred percent," he panted. "But you have one thing backwards, I'm the one who can't believe you're mine." He ran a finger lovingly down her cheek.

Chapter 16

A Charity is formed

Within minutes Rose felt strange. "Simon, I think that regression thing is starting." She rubbed circles on her churning stomach, "Holy cow! Did you see that!?" Her abdomen began to twitch.

"How do you feel? Can I do anything?" His brows were tight with worry.

"It's not too bad and Cade said there wouldn't be anything for you to do but wait. It's only a little crampy but it feels freaky."

"Do you want me to stay or leave? Anna said you had to focus and breathe and I shouldn't distract you." He ran his hands up and down her arms.

"You can stay, so far it's not as bad for me as it was for her. Maybe it's because I don't need to regress as far as she did." A slightly sharper twinge rolled across her stomach then eased a moment later.

"Now that was crazy! Your hair, it looked like it retracted into your scalp."

"I wore it shorter when I was twenty five. Forgot about that." She touched her hair tentatively.

She rocked back and forth on the bed, trying to ease the cramping, as it grew stronger. Dull aches radiated in her knees, and shoulders. Then everything began to tingle all at once like when her foot fell asleep.

"Could you rub my back and kind of all over, my skin is tingling and feels like it needs to be stimulated for blood flow or something."

"Anything I can do, mon amour." He began rubbing small, soothing circles on her back and shoulders.

"How bad is it, Rose?" All Anna said was there would be pain, but not too debilitating, and with breathing it would pass fairly quickly.

"The cramps seem to be over. But my knees, fingers, and toes are hot and achy. Oh shit! That hurts like a mother." Rose grabbed her left arm and rocked as she panted."

Her muscles started to contract and tighten. The sensation felt like right after a heavy workout. Exhausted and invigorated at the same time.

"Tell me the pain is lessening?" he pleaded.

"Actually it is. It's not over but its getting better, the breathing helps."

Okay, shut up and let her concentrate.

Rose laughed and shook her head. "You're so cute."

She was turning her arm this way and that, admiring her leaner, tighter, toned bicep. "Oh my god, look at that." They watched as her skin began to tighten like 3M plastic on a window when you heat it with a hairdryer. She tipped her head back and laughed. "This is great!"

"Hey now! You said you wouldn't get skinnier." He wasn't pleased when her curves started to shrink making her soft, round body trimmer and a bit more lithe. She still had an incredibly curvaceous body as long as the shrinking stopped.

"You big baby, I barely changed at all." She swatted him teasingly. "I think this might be over." She searched her body and held her breath.

He pulled her into his arms. "Let's wait a minute to be sure."

After a minute she wiggled free and slowly stretched on the bed, trying out her new or was it old body. *How do I look?*

His eyes glowed bright as he devoured this new Rose with his gaze. A sexy lopsided grin spread across his face.

"I'm assuming you like what you see."

"Oh, yeah." Simon gave her right nipple a lick. "I think I need to sample my mate inch by inch from head to toe. You know, introduce myself."

Laughing she shoved him over so she could check out her reflection in the bathroom mirror.

"Holy hot momma! I don't remember looking this good, but I'm not complaining."

You are absolutely beautiful. Mon amour. Stunning.

She ran her hands over her perky breasts and down over her round but much smoother hips. Then she touched her hair. That would definitely need to be grown back out. She caressed her cheek with her fingertips, her skin was tight and supple again. She really liked the woman gazing back at her. A lot.

"If the general population knew about this, women everywhere would line up to be matched with a shifter."

He took her by the shoulders and turned her to face him. "I thought you were the sexiest woman I had ever seen before and now you blow my mind. How do you feel?"

"This is the best day ever! I feel amazing."

"What do you think caused the pain in your arm?" he asked.

"Oh, that. I broke it roller blading. It felt like the bone was rebuilding or something. Now that, I can do without ever experiencing again."

"Ditto, I can live with out it too. My wolf was going insane when your pain peaked."

Rose busted out laughing. "You do remember the conversation about this at Cade's right?"

He frowned. "Of course."

She patted his chest. "You are never going to survive being in the room when I give birth, that's for sure."

"I already solved that problem, Cade and Anna can have all the babies." He nodded proudly.

"Um, think again. I plan to have a large family. But right now I'm starved, are you going to feed me mate?" she asked as she flashed him her delectable backside and walked into the bedroom for her clothes.

They moved to the kitchen. "Anything you want, cher. What are you hungry for?" Still naked he wrapped his apron around his waste.

"I could really go for a thick steak and baked potato. OH, and chocolate cake."

He smiled and pulled a steak from the fridge. "That sounds delicious, I'll make two and eat with you."

Simon: Le Beau Brothers

Twenty minutes later her taste buds rejoiced in a state of bliss, everything smelled and tasted better than she ever experienced. "This is the best food I've ever had," she moaned in food ecstasy.

"That's your shifter senses. You'll hear better, smell everything, tastes will be layers now instead of a mixture of flavor, and you'll have perfect night vision. All of the senses I have."

"That reminds me, you never told me what your special gift is."

"I'm an extremely strong empathic. I feel emotions up to ten miles away."

"Oh man, that must really suck sometimes."

"You've no idea."

"I wonder if I'll have a gift?"

"Oh. You will. We just need to wait and see what it is. Do you feel different, other than your new wolf senses, I mean?"

"No, not really."

She put her knife and fork across her plate and dabbed with her napkin. "So, when do I get to learn how to shift?"

"Are you tired at all?"

She frowned at him. "No, why?"

"If you try to shift when you are very tired you can find yourself stuck in wolf form until you have the energy to shift back."

"No worries, I feel fantastic."

He put their plates in the sink and held out his hand. "Then let the shifting begin." He led her into the living room.

She watched him push the furniture to the walls. "I must be shifting into a really large wolf," she teased.

Simon chuckled. "I'd rather be safe than sorry. I'm never sure what you'll do as a human, who knows what you'll try as a wolf." There was a little too much amusement in his eyes.

"Fine, rain on my parade," she teased. "When I've seen you and Anna shift, it just happened. How do I do that?"

"Close your eyes and visualize yourself as a wolf. You don't need to worry about the color and size to do it. You'll naturally become the correct wolf." He took a step out of the circle. "Keep in mind, you need to see yourself as a real live wolf with fur and a tail. Cade didn't tell Anna and she became a wolf in human clothes." He laughed. "I would have loved to see that."

"Got it, fur, tail, no clothes." She closed her eyes.

"Very nice." He said as his eyes consumed her.

Rose stood before him completely naked. "Apparently I was overly focused on the clothing." She closed her eyes again and a beautiful dove grey wolf stood in the center of the room.

Simon gasped. "I should have known," he whispered.

Rose's wolf cocked its head and sat looking at him.

He waved her toward the full-length mirror down the hall. As he walked he stripped off his shirt. "I need you to see yourself."

Rose's wolf frowned and padded after him.

"Stand right there in front of the mirror."

She did as he said and watched as he turned his back to the mirror.

Her wolf yelped in surprise and instantly Rose stood in the room. "What the heck? How am I the tattoo on your back?" She spun to face him.

"Let's sit, this may take a minute."

She sat on the edge of the bed and waited.

"Before Cade and Anna met they had dreams of each other for five years. Very real dreams, visions might be a better word. When I was in the desert I was unable to get the contact and touch that a shifter needs and I suffered for it. Toward the end when it became extremely difficult, I began to have dreams. Every night a dove grey wolf came to me in my dreams and lay beside me to comfort me. I had a local tattoo artist put the wolf on my back as a way to receive some much needed contact as well as a tribute to my savior. I didn't know until a moment ago that you, Rose, were my savior. Your wolf's soul somehow came to me each night when I needed it most."

"Wow."

"Yeah, wow."

"Does that happen a lot? A shifter's mate coming to them before they even meet?"

"No. Actually, I've never heard of it before. Just another unique thing about my mate." He chuckled and took her face in his hands and kissed her.

"I'm not a weird shifter freak, am I?"

"No, cher. You're perfectly normal. I think the wolf Goddess sent your wolf soul to me to help me survive. That lack of contact is what made me so ill. When I came home I shifted to wolf and wasn't able to shift back. Anna worked on healing me for months before you appeared and the rest is history."

"So that's what you guys were talking about."

"Yes, I couldn't explain it to you until you accepted the mating. Humans aren't supposed to know about us."

"Well, if I'm ever going to shift outside I better get this clothing problem handled." She giggled as she looked down at her naked body.

"You should really practice a few more times, I sure don't want Stefan seeing you in your birthday suit. He might get ideas and then I'd have to kill him. My mother wouldn't appreciate that."

She closed her eyes again and breathed deep to relax herself. Next thing she knew she was a wolf again. She wagged her tail and hopped from the bed to nip at his toes.

"Hey, cut that out." He chuckled pulling his feet up. "Now imagine yourself human again but fully clothed."

She stopped teasing and closed her wolf eyes. A second later, Rose stood before him in a sexy sundress from her closet.

"Very good," he reached for her running his palms up her legs to find bare cheeks in his hands. "Uh oh, you forgot your panties."

"No, I didn't," she said biting her lower lip.

His eyes glowed hot and he gave her a love tap on her bare right cheek. "You are terrible to tempt me like that when we have serious work to do. Practice one more time and then we have a date to play pool with Cade and Anna."

Rose closed her eyes… and nothing. "What happened?"

"Nothing, you just need to practice and concentrate. The more you practice the easier it becomes."

A few minutes later Rose's wolf stood before him and gave him a big wolf grin before she shot from the room. He found her in the living room jumping from one piece of furniture to the next. When she spied him she stopped, gave a playful yip and crouched to play. *Want to play with me?* She wiggled her butt in the air still crouching.

"Cher, I'd love to play but we don't have the time, right now. When we get back if you're not too tired we can go for a run and have some fun." He scratched her wolf's ear affectionately. "Now shift back and give me a kiss, woman."

She concentrated and she was a human again, and completely naked. This was going to take a lot of practice.

Simon sank the eight ball for the win. "YES! That's two in a row."

Cade was glowering at his brother, apparently he really didn't like to lose. It didn't help that Stefan had dropped by and had been poking the grumpy wolf with barbs all night.

Anna stepped in. "How about one last game?"

"Yeah, Cade, I want to see Simon and Rose beat you a third time," Stefan teased.

"How about you go home instead," he growled.

"Aww, come on, you big baby," he goaded. "Speaking of babies, how's my nephew doing?"

When he reached for Anna's belly Cade launched himself at him.

Simon struggled to break them apart as Rose squeezed her eyes shut and prayed for the fighting to stop. And for everyone to get along again. She really wanted Cade to be in a better mood.

Suddenly the men stepped back from one another and laughed.

Cade shook his head. "What just happened?"

Simon rubbed his heart. "I have no idea, but I feel great, like I'm crazy happy."

"Yeah," Stefan agreed.

Cade cocked a brow. "Has Rose's gift manifested yet?"

"No, we were just talking about …"

They stopped laughing and turned toward the women.

Anna looked at Rose with her brows raised too.

"What?" she squeaked as she suddenly felt like she was in a spot light.

"Sweetheart, when we were fighting what were you doing?" Simon asked.

"Nothing." She shook her head.

"Were you thinking anything?"

Rose felt the heat rise up her neck to her face. "Yeah, kind of."

"What exactly?"

"I just wanted the fight to stop and for you all to get along." Then she whispered, "And for Cade to be in a better mood."

Simon grinned at her, and the look in his eyes was kind of unnerving.

I want you to try something for me, think that you want Stefan to be really sad.

"That's ridiculous," she protested.

"Please, baby, just do it for me."

She breathed a big sigh and closed her eyes.

A few seconds later, Stefan started to cry. "What did you do?" He glared at Simon through the tears.

"Rose is my mirror opposite. She can control emotions."

"No way!" Rose and Anna said at the same time.

"Yes, way," Simon chuckled.

"Too bad your gift didn't manifest until after the conversion. That would have come in handy against Travis," Stefan sniffled.

"Huh, I wish I'd gotten something cool like Anna did."

"You have no idea how powerful that gift is," Cade said. "You can walk into any situation and change the emotions, effectively changing the minds of any person there."

"Now it sounds kind of creepy," she said with a leery expression.

"Trust me, babe, it will be great." Simon wrapped her in his arms.

Thomas and John walked in from the guest suite wearing serious and determined expressions.

John went to Rose and gave her a hug. "I'm so glad we got you back, Momma Rose."

"I'm glad you're all here. We've decided to petition the wolf Goddess for conversion."

You could have heard a pin drop, no one breathed.

"Are you absolutely sure about this?" Anna asked.

"Yes, we discussed it and decided joining the family completely and moving here is what we want."

"The situation Rose was just in isn't clouding your judgment?" Cade asked.

"That was just one of many factors, I don't care to give a laundry list of reasons. This is what we want. So, what do we have to do?"

"Nothing. I'll tell Emma you've requested the petition and she'll take care of it," Anna assured them.

"Okay, so how long does that take?" John asked.

Cade shrugged. "Don't know. We've never done it before. I guess we'll find out as we go."

"Oh, so now what should we do?" Thomas frowned.

"Stay with us, we can talk to Isaac about work for you and you can decide if you want to build a house here or live somewhere else."

Thomas stuck his hands in his pockets. "That sounds like a plan." He nodded.

He tipped his chin toward the table. "What ya'll got going on here?"

"We're just playing one last game before Simon and Rose head home."

"If you want another game, we will take you on after they leave," John offered.

"Perfect, you guys can re-inflate my manly pride when these two beat me again. Now, how about that game?" Cade said.

Simon: Le Beau Brothers

***

They secretly let Cade win the last game before they went home. They could've won all three games against Cade and Anna, Rose was a regular shark. He'd have to use that against Stefan someday soon and beat him too. Watching him lose to a woman would be priceless. "How are you feeling, cher? Are you tired?"

Rose yawned. "A little."

"Unless you want to spend the night as a wolf I wouldn't chance a shift," he warned.

"I certainly don't want that. I can practice again tomorrow."

Simon held his mate on their newly installed porch swing. The moonbeams shone through the trees, ethereal streams glowing in the darkness. As a human, you couldn't see them so clearly. The night birds were singing, and a light breeze caressed his skin bringing the perfume from the magnolia tree across the yard. Life was pretty great. He rubbed his chin in her silky hair, ran his palm up and down her arm, and pulled her closer.

"Cher, I've been thinking about what I want to do with my time. I don't want to go back to the Le Beau Corporation, at least not, right now."

"What do you want to do?"

"I made a few calls. There is a desperate need for posttraumatic stress disorder dogs and other psychological and physical needs of returning veterans. I'd like to start a charity to help the men."

"That sounds great!"

"Would you be interested in doing that with me?"

She raised her head from his chest. "Really? You want me to help?"

"I won't do it without you, cher."

Snuggling again. "All right, I'm in. What do you want me to do?"

"I'd like to provide trained PTSD dogs free of charge to the men. We'd need to fund their travel and housing expenses for an extensive stay. I think we should consider building a training and housing compound."

"Do you have a property in mind or do we need to see what is available as options? Have you researched or visited existing facilities?"

"I haven't visited any in person, but I've done extensive research. My old commander Mark Anderson just retired and he'd like to work with us. I asked him to visit the top locations and report back to me."

"That's a great idea, we can take the best operations and duplicate or improve on them."

"I'd also like to have a branch of the charity to locate and ship the dogs that soldiers adopt while on deployment home to them. I can't begin to explain how important those dogs are to the men and when they are sent home they have to leave them behind. It's traumatic for both the man and the animal."

"I recently saw a special on television about that. There are people in the war zones who'll locate the dogs and help ship them back. It was forty five hundred dollars per animal. That would be the easiest service to start and could be offered right away."

"Great, let's get that up and running while we put the rest in place. We'll need experienced trainers and psychiatrists at the compound. The men will need medical assistance as well as learning how to handle the dog they'll receive. Plus, applicants will need to be screened for their physical and psychological needs. Every dog will then be trained for their owner's specific disability so it helps its owner with their exact needs. I want to provide the best help while protecting the dog's safety."

"I can look into that and interview candidates," Rose offered.

"Perfect. Eventually I want to expand to physical service dogs and seeing-eye dogs. Mobility service dogs are trained to work with wheelchair-bound clients, walkers, and people with balance issues, things like that. They can even do cool stuff like get the remote or turn off a light. Can you verify the trainer can do all that?"

"Absolutely."

"When we choose a site for the project, I want to leave room for a breeding kennel and puppy building. That way we can pinpoint the perfect breeds and bloodlines we prefer and raise them from birth. I know labradors and golden retrievers are excellent, but I'm sure there are other breeds too."

"I love puppies! So, what does a PTSD dog do?"

"They sense when a person is experiencing panic and alert them to this change in mood. The dogs do this by physically providing a "shield" either in front of or behind the client to make them feel protected. The dogs also nudge their owner or alert them in other tactile ways so the client uses the dog as a comforting presence, stroking the dog or talking to the dog gently.

"I'd like you to organize a fundraising ball to kick off the charity. Your experience and expertise will be invaluable."

"Oh, that sounds like fun! I love organizing fundraisers. Is there a wealth base in the area to support a ten thousand dollar a plate dinner?"

He Laughed. "No problem, there is a lot of money in New Orleans. What about the dance?"

"I'm thinking a glamorous ball, not a costume affair. If we want the big money we need to let them show off their wealth and bling. No hiding behind a mask."

"I like that."

"Do you know many single successful men and women locally?"

"Yeah...why?"

"Have you ever been to a date auction?"

Laughing again. "A what?" His vibrating chest tickled her ear.

"It's an auction where the local men and women agree to be auctioned off for a date. Dinner, dancing, all very respectable."

"Oh, I have one single successful brother you can auction off, right now." Simon grinned.

"I bet you have. Emma and Anna can help me with the auction lineup. You, my love, will need to deliver a wallet pulling speech to promote the project."

"A speech I can do, no problem."

"Combine the plate fee and the money raised from the auction and you'll have a good start."

"How much time will you need to organize this shindig?"

"Provided a venue is available, caterer, musicians…as quickly as four weeks."

"Holy cow, you're fast."

"I've done a hundred of these. They're all pretty much the same."

"Let the planning begin." Simon set his shoulders and took a breath. "Mon amour, I have something else I wanted to talk with you about."

Rose sat up to see him better. "What, babe?"

"I love you with every fiber of my being and I know human women dream of a wedding. Would you like a wedding with your friends and family here to celebrate with you?"

"No." She said without a second of hesitation.

"Really?"

"I only have Anna, Thomas and John as friends and my only family is Jack and Michael. Besides, as far as I'm concerned the mating was much more binding than any marriage could ever be. If for some reason we need to be married then we can do it quietly with a justice of the peace."

"If you're absolutely sure?" He searched her face.

"Absolutely." Smiling, she snuggled again content with the world.

The next morning, Rose was enjoying coffee with her team. "Emma, can you handle the auction singles? You're the only one who has lived here long enough to know the people available."

"I would love to, I have several in mind already."

"Anna, would you work on a list of attendees we

can invite? You have your finger on the pulse of the
business and financial community."

"Piece of cake. Cade can help me."

"I'm going to preview venues, caterers, and the
music options. I'll also need printed invitations, a
decorator, and security."

"Emma, do you think Isaac would be willing to
act as auctioneer?"

"Oh my goodness, he will be tickled you thought
of him."

"Perfect! We don't need a professional auctioneer.
We want someone the people will recognize and enjoy.
Isaac has the perfect combination of celebrity status,
charisma, and humor." Rose was brimming with
excitement. She was in her element.

"Is there anything else we can help with?" Anna
asked.

"Once I have a short list of venues and venders,
I'd love to have you both give your opinions on the
final choices."

"I'm game, Emma gave me a clean bill of health
so I'm no longer tethered to the bed."

"I would be honored. And if you need a printer, I
have a friend who does magical things with calligraphy
and has a top quality shop."

"If she has your endorsement, she's hired." Rose
beamed. "Are you both available to have a coffee
powwow in two days to see where we are at?"

"I am, Cade won't let me leave the house without
him until the threat against us is ended. I'm not allowed
to go to the office so I work from home."

"I have all the time in the world so just let me

know." Emma patted her hand.

Everyone had a task and they were off to a great start.

It had been two weeks of whirlwind planning. Rose blew a strand of hair from her eyes as she reviewed the final list of singles for auction. This was going to be a resounding success. She traded that list for the invitees' roster. Running her finger down the response column she was pleased. There would be three hundred attending and twenty singles auctioned. That would guarantee three million raised plus the auction. *I can't wait to tell Simon.*

He was meeting Mark at the airport and settling him into an extended stay hotel. Once the facility was built, Mark would play a major roll in management and publicity. For now, Simon wanted his input into the bones of the organization. There was no one he trusted more than Mark to help build this service. He had the connections in the military and Washington as well as first hand experience in the needs of a returning vet.

She smiled to herself as she recalled his shining smile when Mark accepted the position of Vice President for The Unforgotten Hero Foundation or TUHF. They had the land purchased and the contractor and architect were working furiously to have designs ready for the kick off ball.

Her heart fluttered when her caller ID read Simon. "Hey, babe, how did it go?"

"Great! Mark looks wonderful, I could barely tell he had a prosthesis. He has a hi-tech design that lets him walk without a cane or anything. I asked him to research providing a service for rehab and custom fitting. How is your day going?"

"Perfect, everything is coming together. Have you heard if the scale model will be ready for display at the ball?"

"They're on track to have it to me a few days before so we can review it ahead of time."

"YES! I really want that on display, it makes the need real for the donators. Did you ask Mark to attend and speak?"

"I went one better, he is now one of your auction singles."

"That's great! The ladies are going to eat him up."

"I have a call coming in. I'll be home in ten minutes. Love you."

"Love you, too."

Everything was ready except her. *Crud, what am I going to wear?*

Chapter 17

The Ball

Rachel Jorgenson's heart pounded as she glimpsed the mile long line of sleek vehicles, each worth more than her house. Her king cab ¾ ton stuck out like a crawfish on a plate of prime rib.

Craning her neck she spotted a hidden area at the back of the lot. She tried to pull out of the line of Bentleys, Mercedes...*Oh my god is that an Aston Martin?* But NO! The man in the orange traffic vest forced her to follow the cars to the valet at the grand entrance. She groaned when the tuxedoed man with white gloves reached for her door handle. *I am so going to kill Emma.* Why the heck did she have to use this as payback for curing her stallion? It made no sense at all.

Come to the ball, it's for a very worthy cause. It'll be fun, Emma had said.

"Fun like a root canal," Rachel grumbled, none too happy Emma failed to mention Stefan, the ego maniac womanizer, would be there.

When she'd first met the Romeo years ago, he'd ignored her completely, never even noticing she was alive. Of course she'd been sixteen and to her he'd looked very mature and manly. *He still could have at least noticed me*, she thought, *or at least acknowledged I was in the room.*

She wasn't sure of the exact date, but about the time of her eighteenth birthday she had even started to have dreams about the infuriating man. Hot dreams. Really hot dreams. And that just pissed her off more.

She bit back a few choice comments she was aching to fling at him. And having grown up with only her father and a few cowboys, they would be juicy words. She hid in a group of attendees. *I'm such a coward.* Even though she was sure he wouldn't know who she was or notice her for that matter, she didn't want him to see her in the spray on gown Emma forced on her. *For fuck's sake, I'm not Madonna or Miley Cyrus. People are going to think I'm walking around wearing pasties in this thing.* She still wondered how Emma had gotten a dress the exact color of her skin with black lace strategically placed.

With her heart heavy, she watched him flirt with a group of beautiful women across the room. Sighing, *why do I let him get to me like this?*

Stefan Le Beau caught the attention of a waiter carrying a tray of champagne and offered the refreshments to a group of ladies. As he greeted each with a smile and a flute of bubbly he realized he had dated each of them in the past six months. Making small talk as he tried to extricate himself from his self-made fiasco, he scanned the room for any women he *hadn't* dated.

He'd barely escaped from the clinging mob of estrogen when Marcus joined him.

"What's with the scowl," his brother asked, gray gaze twinkling with mischief. "Poor, Stefan, already date all the women here?"

Make that *ex*-brother.

"Cute, go find someone else to annoy."

"No, he probably got turned down for the first time in his life and can't handle the shock." Cade said, coming up behind them. "Lose your mojo, Stefan?"

"Up yours. I could get any woman in the room to go home with me, your wife excluded, of course."

Marcus grinned at Cade. "Shall we take bets?"

"Hell, yeah! We'll choose a woman in the room and Stefan has to get her to go home with him."

"Great idea." They were both scanning the room when Cade spied Rachel. He tipped his head in her direction. "The woman in the...is that see through?"

Stefan squinted to see whom he was referring to, the damn room was too dark all he could see was she wore a flesh tone and black lace dress. *Oh, who cared? He would win regardless who she was.* "You're on. If I win you give me your house in the Caymans for a week."

"If we win, you clean the dog kennels for a month at Simon's compound when it's finished." Marcus smirked. He could tell by the gleam in Cade's eye, he recognized Rachel Jorgenson too. She had a reputation for avoiding men, especially handsome men like Stefan. This was going to be fun to watch.

Cade and Marcus laughed and slapped him on the back before leaving him to mingle with the crowd. Stefan scowled at their retreating backs then said, "Bring it on, guys."

Left to his own devices he scanned for the woman who would be his lucky date of the night. Where had that gal in the see-through dress gone anyway?

Rachel walked behind Stefan, making her way through the crowded room. Her heady scent grabbed him by the ears and swung his head around. She held her head high, confidence emanated from every pore. He couldn't see the woman's face, she had already passed him and all he could see was her backside. And what a sweet backside it was. Stefan's mouth watered as her hips swayed. If her scent hadn't been enough to cause and immediate raging hard on, one look at her curvaceous body would have done the trick. Shifting his stance, he was ready to burst the seams of his tuxedo.

Stefan's breath caught in his throat. It's her, the woman his brothers had wagered he couldn't seduce. As the spicy musk scented woman turned slightly, he finally caught a glimpse of her face. His heart accelerated. He had visions of this woman. He didn't dream of her as often as he would like, but he had dreamt of her.

In those visions he had recognized some of the locations they occurred in. It only made sense she might be real and living in the area. He had spent night after night visiting club after club on the off chance she might be in one of them, only to spot her at a charity auction? How bizarre was that? He almost didn't believe it. Could he be that lucky? Cade and Simon had both dreamt of their mates before they met them. Here she was, standing across the room, his vision lover. His MATE.

He set his scotch on the cocktail table next to his elbow and began making his way toward her.

Simon: Le Beau Brothers

She leaned down in order to hear the woman speaking to her. The movement caused her thick chestnut hair to slide over her shoulder. The movement caught the light cast by the chandeliers in the room and made her sleek tresses shimmer. Ah hell, there went his pants again.

As he neared her, he slowed and closed his eyes. He was enveloped in the warm soft cloud of her scent. His heart pounded so hard he expected to see it hanging from his chest.

Slowly, she straightened and turned, frowning into the crowd. It looked as if she was searching for someone. She inhaled a quick breath. A small, rapid movement that was barely discernible. He began to step forward when he felt the sweep of her gaze and stopped in his tracks. He experienced that probing gaze as much as he saw it. Holding his breath, he stood frozen in place. Before he could convince his legs to work again, his mother took her arm and she move away from him. As he watched them cross the room he swore his mother glanced at him with a gleam in her eye. What was up with that?

He raked his fingers through his hair in agitation. The auction was about to begin and everyone was being called to take their seats. Damn it, why did his mother have to show up right when he was about to introduce himself. Signaling a waiter for another scotch, he was going to have a long night and he needed all the help he could get.

A throat cleared, drawing everyone's attention to Simon standing at the microphone with Rose.

"Welcome to the first annual dinner and ball for The Unforgotten Hero Foundation or TUHF (Tuff)." A chuckle rolled across the room. "Please, let me introduce a few key players in the organization. My beautiful Rose is the vice president of events and promotions and the driving force behind tonight's event."

Rose stepped forward and waved to the crowd.

"My old commanding officer Mark Anderson has agreed to be my vice president of operations. Mark, come on out here."

Mark stepped from behind the right side stage curtain and bowed.

"Most of you are aware of my tour of service with the Marines. What you may not know is I had a long road to recovery once I was stateside. The unrelenting love of my family and an incredible woman..."

He drew Rose to his side. "Brought me back to the land of the living. Not all returning veterans are so lucky. My personal experience and the need of these veterans is what fueled the creation of this charity."

He waved Mark onto the stage.

Mark walked to him head held proud. If you didn't know he lost his right leg from the thigh down you wouldn't even catch the slight limp.

As he approached, Simon went ridged, tall and proud, chest out in a perfect salute.

Mark saluted him back then drew him into a back thumping hug.

"Before the evening festivities begin, I would like you to know a bit more about what this foundation provides. I have asked Mark to explain what your donation dollar will offer. Mark, they're all yours."

Mark took the microphone and quietly scanned the crowd, making eye contact here and there. Men began to stand and respectfully salute this retired hero. Slowly, one by one, the room stood and gave a standing ovation to the proud warrior before them.

"Thank you, thank you. I appreciate the warm welcome. So, why are we asking you to loosen your purse strings tonight? What exactly could a dog possibly do for a soldier suffering PTSD? We believe the animal-human bond is an absolutely indisputable part of emotional, mental, spiritual, and physical healing. We are seeking to make this healing available to everyone, regardless of financial or other challenges that might discourage them from seeking this invaluable resource. A service or therapeutic companion dog as they are sometimes called, can help a soldier recover and adjust back into civilian life easier if they are experiencing panic attacks, anxiety, depression, nightmares, flashbacks, or agoraphobia.

"So how will the dog help with these things, you ask? The dog travels beside their owner in public places such as restaurants, grocery stores, buses, etc. helping to ease any anxiety the owner may experience. When in a crowded environment the dog will stay between its owner and any person approaching too close, creating a calm, yet friendly, 'barrier.' The dog will awaken its owner from a nightmare and then calm him. Should the dog sense fear or anxiety, it will try to redirect its owner's thoughts elsewhere."

A dog in a service vest calmly walked onto the stage and stood next to Mark. When he didn't continue the dog nudged his hand to get his attention.

"Pardon me, this is my service dog, Rizzo."

The crowd gave a rousing applause for Rizzo.

"What I've described is just the tip of the iceberg of what a service animal can do for the victims of PTSD. Studies show that up to eighty percent of patients show marked improvement once they receive their dog."

He paused for a moment to take a sip of water. "So, how long does it take to train a dog to do incredible things like I have laid out? Generally nine months. This includes: twice-a-week training for six months, followed by supplemental mentoring sessions. Both dog and man will need a bit of training.

"I was going to recount a success story of a friend of mine but perhaps I'll save that for another day. I'd like to leave you with the knowledge that for every forty thousand dollars raised, we can provide one soldier with a quality of life they would otherwise never have. These men sacrificed for freedoms we take for granted every day, it's our turn to sacrifice for them. Thank you."

Mark saluted the crowd and walked off the stage with Rizzo.

Simon returned to the stage. "Thank you, Mark, and how about his awesome dog, Rizzo." The crowd clapped their appreciation. "Now it's time for the auction. Twenty-one local professionals and celebrities have volunteered to be our auction items tonight. If you are the lucky bidder, you'll win a dinner date with your prize. You'll also have a dance partner for the ball, if you so desire. Let me be very clear, there is no hanky panky favors involved in winning one of the singles." A chuckle rose from the audience. "With no further ado, I give you our auctioneer, Isaac Le Beau."

Isaac took the stage to a rousing standing ovation. "Thank you, you're too kind. Let me start the auction with a man you have already met tonight, Mark Anderson."

The crowd applauded for him again then settled down for the fun and serious business of one-upping their neighbor. Mark was won by a pretty fifty something woman and seemed very pleased with his date.

The auction continued and an hour into the bidding the woman in the see through dress took the stage. Stefan couldn't breathe. *YES she's mine!* It didn't matter if bidding went to a million dollars he was winning this beauty.

"Ladies and gentlemen, let me introduce Rachel Jorgenson. Rachel owns the Shadow Hill Stables. She is also a respected large animal veterinarian. Who will start the bidding at ten thousand dollars?"

A man in the front raised his hand.

"I have ten, now eleven to the man in the back, twelve to you." He gestured to the man in the front row.

The gentleman nodded.

"I have twelve, now thirteen to the man by the wall. Who will give me fourteen?"

Stefan couldn't take it, "Twenty thousand," he yelled from the middle of the room.

Rachel gasped and wobbled on her skyscraper high heels.

"I have twenty from my son, Stefan, who will go twenty one?"

The man in the back raised his hand again.

Shit! He would not let another man win his mate.

"Twenty one to you, Sir, twenty two?"

The man along the wall raised his hand and stared directly at Stefan defiantly.

Oh hell, no. "Fifty thousand," Stefan yelled while never breaking eye contact with the dandy along the wall.

Rachel had to grab Isaacs arm to steady herself. *What is he doing?*

"Sixty thousand," came from along the wall.

Rachel's head was swimming.

"Are you okay?" Isaac whispered. "Here, take a sip of water and a deep breath."

She took a deep breath and a large gulp of water. *Nope, didn't help.*

Stefan growled at his nemesis across the room. Cade patted his arm, "Cool it, brother, not in public."

"One hundred thousand," he challenged.

Rachel stumbled and Simon rushed unto the stage with a chair. She sat shaking in front of three hundred people. *Just shoot me and get it over with.*

"I have one hundred, bids to you, Sir." Isaac gestured to the man along the wall.

He glared at Stefan for a few seconds then shook his head.

"I have one hundred, going once…going twice…"

"One hundred ten," the stranger in the rear of the

room yelled.

Stefan literally snarled in frustration. He wasn't used to being denied what he wanted. Having finally found his mate, experiencing the happiness his brothers had was within his grasp. This bidding war was frustrating as hell.

Stefan stood and slowly turned to face the man, "Two hundred thousand," he said in an eerily calm voice.

"What are you doing?" Rachel yelled at him. Then clapped her hand over her mouth.

Isaac chuckled, "I have two hundred to, Stefan, do I hear three?"

The audience chuckled.

"Two hundred once...two hundred twice...two hundred thousand to Stefan Le Beau."

The crowd cheered and clapped loudly.

Isaac looked to his wife standing in the wings and gave her a triumphant wink. He watched as Emma clapped happily.

Rachel hid her face in her hands. She jumped when Simon touched her arm to help her from the stage. *Emma was a dead woman.*

Forty five minutes later the auction was finally over. Thank god, she could finally go home. Her feet were swollen and something was doing a tap dance on the inside of her skull. The Tylenol she took fifteen minutes ago hadn't kicked in yet. She rubbed the edge of her sole, should she chance taking the shoe off? *Crud, I might not get it back on. Then what? Go bare foot in this gown?* That wouldn't be embarrassing, not at all.

Rachel stood and limped to the door leading to the ballroom. She groaned as she looked at the crowd she had to walk through to get to her truck. This was going to be a thousand times worse than a walk of shame. She giggled at her bad pun. Yeah, she was losing it.

"What's so funny?"

The deep timber of his drawl had no business sending her pulse racing. "Nothing." She squared off with Stefan. "Were you dropped on your head as a child?"

He frowned. "No."

"Is there a history of insanity in your family?"

"No." He scowled. "What are you getting at?"

"No one in his right mind would bid two hundred thousand dollars. That leaves one conclusion, you're insane."

"Oh, I'm insane all right. Insane for you."

"Right. Go fishing with those lines somewhere else, this woman isn't biting."

"Oh, cher, you wound me." He laid his hand across his heart.

"Shut up, Le Beau." She tried to push past him but he didn't budge. "Please move out of the way."

The band began to play a romantic waltz.

"I do believe they're playing our song." He presented his hand to her.

"What are you doing now?"

"I'm asking the single woman I won at the auction to dance. That is my right as the winner." He winked.

"You're kidding, right?"

"I've never been more serious, I assure you. Now, may I have this dance?" His hand remained extended as he waited for her response.

"Oh, all right. I suppose I have to."

Stefan led her to the dance floor and took her into his arms. She was perfect. His wolf howled in triumph. Now if he could only get her to actually like him.

About the Author

V.A. Dold is the author of the **Le Beau Brothers** series, New Orleans wolf shifter novels. A graduate of Saint Cloud University, she majored in marketing with a minor in reading romance paperbacks.

Prior to becoming a full time writer, she was Publicist to the authors, owning Innovative Online Book Tours and ARC Author & Reader Con's (ARC NOLA) (ARC Phoenix). Still is. The companies mesh well, much like PB&J.

Her idea of absolute heaven is a day in the French Quarter with her computer, her coffee mug, and the Brothers, of course.

A Minnesota native with her heart lost to Louisiana, she has a penchant for titillating tales featuring sexy men and strong women. When she's not writing, she's probably taking in a movie, reading, or traveling.

Her earliest reading memories are from grade school. She had a major fixation with horses, and the Black Stallion was a favorite. Then junior high came along and teenage hormones kicked in. It became all about the Harlequin Romances. She has been hooked on romances ever since.

Connect with V.A. Dold:

Visit V.A.'s website http://www.vadold.com/
Like on Faceboook at
https://www.facebook.com/pages/VA-
Dold/1404660546458551?ref=hl

Follow on twitter at https://twitter.com/

Goodreads
https://www.goodreads.com/user/show/5356266-v-a-
dold

Read on for an excerpt from V.A. Dold's Next book:

Stefan
Book 3 of the Le Beau Brothers

The Plan

Anna Le Beau knocked on her mother-in-law's back door then absently began wringing her hands again. Her heart was in her throat, brow glistening with sweat. Ever since her sons Thomas and John James requested to be converted, she'd been on an emotional rollercoaster.

The door swung open presenting Emma Le Beau's gorgeous smile. "Anna! What a wonderful surprise. I was pouring a cup of tea, would you like one?"

"Good morning. Yes, a cup would be lovely." It would give her hands something to do, anyway. Anna took a seat at the kitchen table to watch Emma pour the tea.

Emma gave her a long look. "They finally asked didn't they?" Her bangles tinkled as she set the cups on the table.

"You know, it is truly creepy sometimes. You know everything before anyone says a word."

"Oh, darlin', not everything. Them boys of mine got away with plenty." Emma patted her hand.

Anna shivered. "I can imagine. No, don't tell me. I'm not sure I even want to know."

Emma threw back her head and laughed. "So, what would you have of me, sweetheart?"

"My boys came to us last night. They've thought it through and would like you to petition the Goddess for their conversion. Tell me this isn't dangerous."

"Oh, heavens no. About a hundred and fifty years back, a man in Omaha requested conversion and it went very smoothly. Keep in mind, the Goddess may decline the request."

Anna sat back in her chair and visibly relaxed. "Thank goodness. I didn't get a lick of sleep over this. So, what do we have to do?"

"Nothing. I will make the request this afternoon during meditation and then we wait."

"Oh. I sure feel silly now. I was all worked up for nothing."

Emma sipped her tea. "Leave everything to me, child. You just take care of my grandchild, ya hear."

Anna finished her tea, feeling much more relaxed than twenty minutes ago. *I really could use a nap.* "Thank you, Momma Le Beau. Please let me know as soon as the Goddess makes her decision."

"Of course, I will. Now, you run on home and take a nice nap. And don't worry about a thing."

Four hours later, Emma knelt before her altar as she prepared for her daily meditation time to speak with the spirits. She drew a calming breath. It wasn't every day a worshipper requested a human conversion.

Simon: Le Beau Brothers

She lit her candles and incense, closed her eyes, and laid her hands palm up in her lap.

"My child, your visits lighten my heart," the Goddess quietly spoke.

"If it pleases you, I humbly request a conversion on behalf of your beloved daughter Anna. She asks that her two human sons be converted to shifter."

"Ah, Thomas and John. Both good, honorable men. Even as humans, they have served me well by protecting my daughter from harm. I grant the request of John James to take place during the next new moon. But, I have other plans for Thomas James."

Emma bowed her head low. "Thank you, mother Goddess. If it pleases you, may I enquire about my sons' mates?"

A soft chuckle sounded from the wavering image. "Your second eldest son has much to learn and his mate will teach him. Her name is Rachel Jorgenson, owner of the Shadow Hill Stables. She will participate in Simon's auction. Take care, my daughter, blessed be."

She watched her slowly fade. *Oh goodness, this is going to take some planning.*

That evening, Emma invited Cade and Anna and her boys to join her and Isaac on the deck. Sweet tea filled her pitcher on the sideboard, adding to the cooling breeze coming off the river. A secret little smile lit her face and her toes tapped a happy rhythm on the decking.

"Are you going to keep me waiting all night, Emma?" Isaac asked with a grin of his own.

She clapped excitedly. "I received answers from the Goddess. She has given me the identity of Stefan's mate. Rachel from the Shadow Hill Stables. She will be at the ball Simon and Rose are hosting and I already have a plan to get her there. I have other news but you have to wait for the others then I will tell everyone."

Isaac scowled playfully and sipped his tea. A few minutes later, footsteps were heard on the wooden planks.

"OH! Here they are." She rushed to hug everyone. Even Thomas wore a grin at her exuberance.

"Hi, Mother." Cade spun her playfully in a circle.

"Oh, you." She gave him a swat and offered tea before settling to serious business.

Five faces stared at her in expectation. "I'm sure you already guessed I have news. John, your request will be granted at the new moon. And Thomas, the Goddess told me she has plans for you as well but she has not disclosed what they are. She never does anything without a very good reason or behaves in a spiteful manner. I am sorry, but you will have to be patient. She did tell me you were both honorable men and were serving her well."

Anna's hand clamped over her mouth. "So fast?"

"When the Goddess makes a decision there is no reason to wait. I will teach you the ritual and we will do it together." She patted Anna's hand.

"Cher, it will be fine. There's nothing to fear, remember?" Cade wrapped his arms around her.

"I know, it's these stupid hormones. Just ignore me."

Simon: Le Beau Brothers

We have fifteen days to prepare. Tomorrow we will go over the ritual and prayers. We will also need to check the herb cabinet to verify we have everything." Emma was all business when it came to her rituals and magic.

"Let me know when you need me to be here."

"This is going to be great!" John shot a look at Thomas and received a toast from his brother for his success.

"I would still like to remain here in New Orleans and live on the plantation if that is okay with everyone." Thomas looked like a kicked puppy.

"Of Course you will," Isaac nodded. "I have plans for you myself. Can you meet with me in the morning?"

"Certainly," Thomas replied.

Everyone celebrated for a few more hours before each sought the comfort of his or her own bed.

34311158R00167

Made in the USA
Lexington, KY
31 July 2014